PRAISE

"By expertly weaving   1e
figure of Vinueza, the   ial
candidate who resembles so many corrupt (but wealthy!)
presidential candidates in the modern history of Ecuador, Gabriela Alemán depicts with verve and humor the horrors and absurdities of a society intent on perpetuating itself."

—Mauro Javier Cardenas, author of
The Revolutionaries Try Again

"Gabriela Alemán has a rhythm worth watching . . . she does something unexpected, things fly apart, she leaps into the void, and you think, 'there's no way she can pull this off'—but no, everything fits together, falls into place, flows, and the story goes on."

—Pedro Mairal, author of
The Missing Year of Juan Salvatierra

"*Poso Wells* is ironic, audacious, and fierce. But what is it, exactly? A satire? A sci-fi novel? A political detective yarn? Or the purest reality of contemporary Latin America. It's unclassifiable—as all great books are."

—Samanta Schweblin, author of *Fever Dream*

"Through scalding wit and straight-faced parody this no-holds-barred absurdist adventure that seems more a movie than a book will have you laughing till you cry as the cruelty of its South American reality sinks in. Imagine a mix of Hunter S. Thompson and Gabriel García Márquez. A small masterpiece."

—Michael Taussig, author of *Beauty and the Beast*

POSO
WELLS

POSO WELLS

Gabriela Alemán

Translated from the Spanish by Dick Cluster

City Lights Books | San Francisco

Cover and book design by Linda Ronan

Library of Congress Cataloging-in-Publication Data
Names: Alemán Salvador, María Gabriela, 1968- author. | Cluster, Dick,
1947- translator.
Title: Poso Wells / Gabriela Alemán ; translated by Dick Cluster.
Other titles: Poso Wells. English
Description: San Francisco : City Lights Books, 2018. |
Identifiers: LCCN 2018000978 (print) | LCCN 2018008832 (ebook)
| ISBN
9780872867819 | ISBN 9780872867550
Subjects: | GSAFD: Suspense fiction.
Classification: LCC PQ7889.2.A438 (ebook) | LCC PQ7889.2.A438
P6713 2018
(print) | DDC 863/.64—dc23
LC record available at https://lccn.loc.gov/2018000978

City Lights Books are published at the City Lights Bookstore
261 Columbus Avenue, San Francisco, CA 94133
www.citylights.com

CONTENTS

For three hours now, he's been sitting on one of the four benches that face the statue of García Moreno in the park between the Basilica and Calle Vargas in the center of the capital city, waiting for Salém's call. Meanwhile, he's been slowly eating his way through the bag of mangoes he bought for a dollar on the corner, watching the people come and go, reminding him of ants. By now, he's sucked the juice from half of the mangoes. He's saturated with the cloying sweetness of the fruit, his hands are sticky, and he's desperately tired. He hasn't slept in two weeks, ever since he promised his mother on her deathbed he'd stop drinking. Maybe he's been waiting for the call here rather than in the streets by the courthouse because, close to the church, something might come along to solve his problems, some divine intervention perhaps. In his shirt pocket he's got an image of St. Expeditus right next to his cell. When the phone finally rings he ignores the sound and continues sucking. With four dead bodies and no arrest, Salém ought to build him a monument. He didn't want to kill her, the judge, not over a land dispute with a drug kingpin rotting in jail. During one of his sleepless nights he'd heard a psychoanalyst on the radio talking about how men who mistreat women have homosexual tendencies. He doesn't want to be remembered as a faggot as well as a murderer. He stands up and walks toward the door of the Basilica, which is unusually packed.

"What's going on here?" he asks a shoeshine boy. He's short of breath and sounds like an asthmatic dog.

"The Jericho pilgrimage," the boy says, knocking twice on the tip of the man's shoe.

Richard Zambrano looks at the boy. He puts one foot on top of the case full of cans of polish and dirty flannel cloths, while drying his sticky hands on his pants. On a flat sheet of rusted steel, the boy mixes some brown polish with a mustard-colored one.

"The what?" Richard asks.

"It starts here and ends there." The shoeshine boy points toward El Panecillo, the breadloaf-shaped hill topped with a statue of the Virgin. "They say you get two wishes if you make it all the way up."

"Yeah?" the man says, interested.

The boy nods and taps the tip of the shoe again. The man switches feet. When the boy is done, Richard tosses a fifty-centavo coin in the air and takes off running after the pilgrims.

PART ONE

THE
COOPERATIVE OF
POSO WELLS

The Candidate

Poso Wells does not appear on any map. How could it? The last time anyone did a topographical survey, that huge mass of mud dredged from the estuary was still part of the river. And water flows. It's not subdivided into lots. But there lies Poso Wells, objections be damned. If you were to ask any of its residents for a precise description of its location, they might tell you it's the most stinking, forgotten hole on this side of the Pacific. Kilometers and kilometers of houses built of sticks and reeds held together by a mix of mud and stones, all resting on a suspension of sewage and moldy clay. Mangrove posts sunk into soft, unstable soil that cracks open in new places with every tide or current sweeping the high-tonnage ships toward the port of Guayaquil. But if that answer didn't satisfy you, and you were to press on with, "But what street do I take, what corner do I turn, from the Beltway do I head north or south?" then most likely you'd be told to go to hell, and your respondent might mutter under her breath that anyone's idea of hell on a bad day would look a lot like Poso Wells. It's in the mouth of the fucking devil, if you really want to know.

And yet, though no one who didn't live there would venture within a hundred yards of that place, when campaign time rolls around it suddenly turns into an electoral battlefield—because there are hundreds of thousands of votes to be had. Every inhabitant needs something, and offers come raining down. Especially housing. Houses are promised in exchange for votes, as are construction materials and building loans. Stages are erected, loudspeakers are hung, and along come the girls, immodestly clothed teenagers who have to be escorted by bodyguards because everyone wants a piece of them. Hundreds of thousands of hands, like tentacles, try to touch them on their way in. But once on stage, that sensation of being mauled fades away. The plaza is electrifying. The girls quickly forget that without the bodyguards, if the stage were to collapse, none of them would survive. They'd be lost in the labyrinthine twist and turns of the barrio, destroyed, only bits and pieces of them to be found. But not this time. Every four years, or sometimes every two, television crews descend on the barrio. Trucks full of cables and satellite dishes arrive. An entire brigade of national police is deployed while a city tractor fixes the roads, or at least fills them with enough dirt from the nearby Santa Elena peninsula to allow the entry of the candidates and their vehicles full of political party boosters and functionaries. In Poso Wells such gatherings always take place on a particular vacant lot, an enormous abandoned rectangle situated in the third phase of the Cooperative, that is, the third part, historically speaking, to be occupied by a wave of settlers. Nobody, in twenty-some years of democracy enacted via repeated election campaigns, has stopped to ask why no houses have been built on this lot, why it doesn't even serve as a sandlot for sports, while elsewhere in the barrio any vacant expanse is invaded by squatters, one lot after another, by settlers who risk their lives to build on top of garbage that has only achieved the flimsiest hold on the riverbed. Why, even though this lot is surrounded by the only lampposts in all of Poso Wells, does no one ever gather there except at campaign time?

The answer is not very interesting—and even less so for those who are charged with the task of covering the news. Those who live in the Cooperative know that something isn't right, but they are not likely to explain. If forced to say what it is about this particular patch of sterile and cursed ground, they couldn't. They simply know, everyone knows, that certain parcels must be avoided. Because all over the barrio, things disappear. A bunch of bananas can't be left outside the door, because it will vanish. It has to be safeguarded inside the house, though padlocks are not much use either. Something crouches in the streets of Poso Wells, and it attacks the nerves like a persistent drumbeat. Whatever it is haunts the dreams of the residents, panting in their faces, slobbering them with noxious saliva and septic-tank breath, leaving their bodies sticky and dirty when they wake up. This sensation of danger cannot be shaken off by a mere act of will. The residents live with it all day long. In the evening it just becomes more palpable, because what vanishes then is not just food. People disappear, too.

At campaign time, the threat diminishes. There are too many electric wires, too many workers, too much equipment turning everything upside down. The music reverberates as the girls dance their way through choreographed moves again and again, though they've been selected for their looks, not their skill. They put on their best faces for the cameras and smile.

In 2006, the campaign in Poso Wells has picked up steam. The first round is over and the winner, who has edged ahead of his opponent by four percentage points, needs to make the next encounter with the electorate more spectacular than the one before. He arrives in a chartered helicopter under the last rays of the late-afternoon sun. The light is diaphanous, ethereal, seemingly infinite as it reflects off the shell of the aircraft. The occupant is as eye-catching as the machine that bears him: Chinese silk guayabera, creamy linen pants that flutter around his gym-toned legs, iguana-skin shoes custom-made in Italy. Long, curly hair falls to his shoulders and down his back, while prominent cheekbones accent his rugged face. His movements are graceful, in the way of those favored by divine Providence or an overstuffed bank account. He isn't tall, but on the stage he'll look enormous. He'll offer to fulfill desires and confer salvation. This time, like every time, he has ordered sacks of cornmeal and flour to be distributed, along with containers filled with lard. While he's still hovering over the cityscape, his boosters distribute these gifts in the plaza. That's why a crowd has piled into the space that had been cleared for the helicopter to land, and now the pilot doesn't know what to do. The candidate sweats, prodigiously, soaking his clothes and tracing a design of wispy wings down the back of his guayabera while he wipes his face with an impeccable handkerchief. He has six more of these waiting in the back pocket of his trousers. Before boarding the copter, he fortified himself with two large bottles of beer and five glasses of whiskey, one after another, at the headquarters of his political party. Now he needs to urinate. Desperately. But, flying over the vast spread of the barrio, he tries to forbear.

"Motherfucker, I can't hold it any more. Get those people out of the way!"

"How?" the pilot asks.

"Get down lower and give it a try," the candidate responds, barely moving his lips and blinded by sweat. "Where there's a will there's way." He takes a deep breath and repeats the adage like a mantra—"Where there's a will, there's a way"—while the pilot nods and attacks the sea of bodies.

But try as he might, no one moves. What do they care if the rotor blades cut off their heads? In the whirlwind, matchbook houses tremble and threaten to fall. The blades cut through TV antennas and pirate electrical wires. On the fourth try, the pilot swoops down close to the designated rectangle while lowering an aluminum ladder, the only way to deposit the candidate on the ground. Under the continuous rush of wind, seven houses perched on rotten posts collapse, accompanied by the crying of children and the screams of women, while husbands and boyfriends try to pull themselves and the women and children from the rubble. But all of this can barely be heard as the loudspeakers saturate the atmosphere with decibels. It's as if the doors of heaven had opened for celestial choirs and trumpet blasts, for all the angels of heaven to proclaim the second coming of the Lord. On stage, the girls shake their hips with frenetic, hypnotizing rhythm. The people shout, jump, sway, swing. No one can hear the protests of those who have just lost their homes. The candidate, his hands spread like a man on the cross, descends through space—the crush around him acts in his favor now—until he touches the earth where his waiting bodyguards surround him. From the viewpoint of the great mass of people, he seems to levitate as the bodyguards lift him bodily to the stage. That's when he realizes he has no place to discharge his bladder in peace. He sweats and sweats, with few options left. He is going to pee, and he's going to do it in front of the hundreds of inhabitants of Poso Wells. He'll be discreet, he'll allow a stream of urine to slide down his linen pants while he moves about the stage to avoid forming a puddle under his feet. In the heat, what his clothes absorb will evaporate quickly. The rest will slip though the gaps in the stage. While he struts about and waves to the clamoring crowd, he puts this plan into action, until his party loyalists close around him in a great human chain and someone hands him a microphone. The electricity can be felt in the air. At this moment, he stops moving and the puddle at his feet takes on a certain depth. It wouldn't bother him, no one would notice it, really, except that he is holding a cable connected directly to one of the high-voltage streetlights, and he's standing in a pool of liquid.

Bad combination.

Before the wires explode and the lights go out—the lights that the organizers of the event have stolen from the lampposts erected by the municipality a few months before—the people see the candidate rise above the stage, encircled by a celestial halo. The glow shoots like lightning through all of his entourage.

Really, it's a sight to behold. Of a strange, extreme beauty. Extraordinarily so.

And then, a smell of meat on the grill. A stench of scorched flesh that permeates every square inch of the usually vacant lot.

And then, finally, pitch black.

Yesterday's papers

He came in search of clues for an article about the disappearances, which had happened months before he arrived. When he realized what a large and difficult task it was going to be, he decided to meet with his editors to ask for more time to investigate and more column inches for his story. The answer was no to both requests. All that had been reported on TV so far was that three or four people, all of them women, had disappeared near the island called Trinitaria in the so-called Cooperative of Poso Wells. It didn't take long for him to discover a lot more: that there was a pattern dating back at least fifteen years, and the number of women who had disappeared was not four but nearly fifty. All this was buried in a tangle of half-finished legal procedures and official neglect: cases never filed, no money to pursue them, dead ends, leads never followed, no clear priorities established, migrants who went back to where they had come from, leaving the names of daughters, wives, and nieces forgotten on the shores of the saltwater estuary. But now, in light of the most recent events, everything that went on in Wells needed to be reevaluated.

Varas had managed to reconstruct those events, in a rudimentary way at least: The candidate who'd won the first round of the elections had been incinerated in a flash, along with all of his possible replacements except one, the lone survivor, who had either been kidnapped or disappeared in the confusion and chaos that ensued. Thus, Varas had the story of the year in his hands. Because of the blackout, the TV cameras had no footage, while Varas—who had asked to cover the rally—had been right there on the stage. He sold the article under any number of pen names to whatever media outlets wanted to buy it, and he proposed to his own paper that they allow him to investigate the disappearance of the late candidate's only possible successor. This time, the owners of the paper did not hesitate to offer him whatever he needed. The story was not missing women, but the country's future. The opposing candidate was already proclaiming his victory, while the Congress met with a slew of legal advisors to try and figure out what procedures to follow. Meanwhile, the charbroiled candidate's backers had thrown their unconditional support behind the missing man—whom, furthermore, they considered anointed by fate. Having narrowly cheated death, he was destined to chart the country's future. At this point, his image was for sale at every stoplight in every city, on every corner throughout the land.

If only people knew what's hidden behind the image of a saint.

Gonzalo Varas had engaged in a bit of distortion, or to put it another way, he had allowed himself certain liberties in the articles he wrote for the nation's serious papers. Serious in the sense that no one dared to impugn anyone's honor, much less that of a dead man. A man who, furthermore, had won the first round of the elections and, even after death, enjoyed political power and connections. But, for the popular daily of the country's principal port, he had described the events that led to the death of eleven people and the disappearance of the twelfth in absolute detail:

MEN WITHOUT EYES

On the night of October 16, to the astonishment of the thousands gathered for a political rally held to celebrate the winning candidate's victory in the first round of the elections, a series of gruesome events resulted in the death of eleven individuals in an unprecedented case of spontaneous combustion. The confusion that followed was rendered even more strange by the appearance of a group of three to five eyeless men who carried off the lone survivor of the electrical short-circuit. When the candidate took to the stage—after nine p.m., with a splendid full moon illuminating the night of our Pearl of the Pacific, also dubbed by the incomparable Daniel Santos the balmy Carribean's farthest port—all those present onstage, the author of this article included, opened a circle to make room for him to, presumably, place himself in the center. The truth is that we did so, without any spoken agreement, because the candidate was sweating like a condemned man and the stench from his armpits could be discerned from some distance away. One could confidently claim that he smelled of death and that his perspiration was mixed with the stink of fear. What could the candidate have been afraid of? This we will never know. What we do know, because I could smell it and see it, is that the candidate began to wet himself in full public view while the organizers introduced him to the public and the dancers performed pirouettes that exposed their nubile, luscious legs. He did not do so like any ordinary man of the people, opening his fly and holding his organ while emptying his bladder; no, what he did was use his leg as a urinal and the stage as a drain—leaving his respect for the noble electorate in some doubt. But, in any case, he walked about the stage while he peed. And let me testify that he peed a lot. And continued sweating. The ensuing vapors caused me to retreat to the farthest corner of the stage, for which I should thank him, because otherwise I might not be here to write these lines. At this point, I must also explain that the candidate did not bring a generator with him, but rather stole the current from some lampposts located about fifteen meters from the stage, by means of two thick cables connected directly to the spotlights and the sixteen loudspeakers which would, in normal circumstances, have left us hypnotized and deaf.

At a certain moment, the rally's announcer went silent, and so did the music—think (because advertisement of commercial recordings is not permitted in this space) of a prime example of reggaeton, of the song most heard today on the airwaves, the one that ironically refers to a highly explosive product that is not diesel fuel—and the announcer approached the candidate, requiring him to interrupt his pilgrimage around the stage. Just for an instant, shall we say, but that was long enough for a puddle of urine to form at his feet. In that instant, there was a sudden loss of current, a drop in voltage. A circuit within the microphone being passed from announcer to candidate let loose a spark. Remember that the candidate was sweating copiously and that salt water is a superb conductor of electricity. It should also be clarified that the spectacle was especially dazzling because current taken from a streetlight is 220 volts, not 110, and because the electricity not only flowed through the drops of sweat on his hand but also rose up like a charmed cobra along the thread of urine running down his leg. According to the coroner's report, the candidate was not just electrocuted but incinerated. When he collapsed, smoke rose from his body. According to the same report, he had a hole in his stomach.

I would speculate that an electrical charge came snaking up from his penis to his other vital organs, causing them to burn to a crisp. What a spectacular departure! The rest of the event was less electrifying. The other members of his party had only a few seconds, as could be seen from the look of terror in their eyes, to realize that death awaited them too. Some tried to let go of each others' hands, to save themselves from an end that would show solidarity, yes, but would otherwise be foolish. But the current was already whisking them off, each one passing it along to the next.

At this point you must be asking, but what about the man who managed to save himself? This man—a chubby man with scarcely any neck, with the face of a frog and the arms of a child—had never joined hands with the others. He was behind a loudspeaker, not very far from me, holding a gold credit card near one of his nostrils. He did not even know what had occurred. When he turned around and saw his comrades, still holding hands, collapsed on the floor among bolts of electricity that snaked around the stage, he managed only to open his mouth and then to cover it with his childlike hand before a group of men, either with no eyes at all or with deeply sunken eyelids, took hold of him and carried him off before he could protest. How did I see this? Thanks to the light of the magnificent full moon shining down on the stage at that moment, only to, lamentably, disappear behind a cloud within an instant.

That was all that was known. And, despite entire battalions of the national army that descended on Poso Wells, nothing more had been found. Not a trace of the missing man. As if he had never existed. Meanwhile, Varas asked questions, walked the streets, and although he did not find anything to lead him to the politician, he continued to accumulate information for his other story, the one about the missing women. He kept finding someone who knew someone who had lost a daughter or a niece. The women vanished like smoke, and no one with the power to do anything seemed to care. Varas decided that his best bet was to find someplace in the barrio to stay, so as not to miss any detail. In his wanderings he met a man named Jaime Montenegro who proved welcoming. Montenegro was an elderly resident with a friendly face, a short, small man who lived alone and had an extra room that he offered to rent to Varas when the reporter told him what he was doing. So he moved in. In the evening, when Varas returned because it was no longer advisable to be walking the dirt streets of Wells, his host would set out two chairs at the entrance to the house and they would talk till nightfall. In these conversations, Jaime told Varas he could no longer even remember when he'd first come to this part of the city, but he did remember that he'd had no neighbors at the time. There'd been no one around but himself and his dog. As a curious note, he remembered a journalist who had showed up around that time to ask strange questions about blind men who came from a valley in the sierra. Jaime had been barely twenty, and so his memory of this was vague. That was the first time, though, that he heard the name of Wells, from the mouth of this same journalist, and he also remembered vaguely that something or other had happened which led to the barrio taking on that name, Poso Wells—or Wells' Sediment in less poetic terms. The "Cooperative" came later, when a savings bank opened and the name appeared on a sign. Later, at the time of the squatters' invasions amidst a clamor for land, a lawyer saw that sign, which was how the name became known outside the neighborhood. Jaime also told Varas that at this time—maybe a decade after his arrival—the first of the women disappeared without leaving a trace. He had lost all track of how many disappearances had occurred since. Everything Montenegro told Varas was invaluable, though it was also clear the old man's memory was a minefield. Varas felt his way through that territory little by little, seeking a path along which Jaime could move forward without his memories exploding in mid-sentence.

"What did that newspaperman want to know?"

"The one from years ago, or the one who showed up here the day before yesterday?"

"The one from when you had just recently come to Wells."

"I told you, he wanted to know if I'd seen a bunch of blind men around here anywhere."

"And had you?"

"No. Really, I hadn't."

"What was the newspaperman's name?"

"He didn't tell me and I didn't ask, but he said a lot of words in another language, and he had a strange accent too. And, like I told you, he was the first one to mention this Wells."

"Who was he?"

"The newspaperman?"

"No, the other guy, Wells."

"A historian, I think. He'd written I-don't-know-what about Ecuador, something that the newspaperman was interested in."

Since Varas wasn't making much progress in the rest of his investigations, he decided to follow the trail of Wells. In the Rolando library, in the center of Guayaquil, he found what he was looking for. It was a book of travel writings by an Englishman who had been in Ecuador toward the end of the nineteenth century. They were impressions, rich in detail, mostly about the central valley of the Andes. They mentioned Guayaquil only as the port where the author landed, but they did discuss a village of blind men and a mysterious encounter with them. Varas made a copy of this chronicle and continued to search for any trace of the other writer, presumably British as well, in papers from the 1950s, when Montenegro had arrived. After three fruitless days in the library, he found an article in the daily *El Telégrafo* signed by someone called Binns. It was neither a news article nor an opinion column, exactly, but more of a collection of fragmentary facts that gave the impression of having been written in the hope that some reader would come forward with more information, which the last paragraph of the article, in fact, openly requested. In the meantime, what Binns said began to give shape to the few things that Varas knew. As if Binns had written the article expressly for him to read fifty years later.

THE END OF A CIVILIZATION?

The first conjectures about the population of the Valley of the Fallen date from the sixteenth century and the alliances that certain Andean potentates sought with the Spaniards, especially the chief called Sancho Hacho, from Latacunga. In spite of his attempts to avail himself of an alliance with the invaders, they came to exercise military control over most of that territory between 1573 and 1597. However, some indigenous groups decided to withdraw to areas still unbeknownst to the new conquerors, areas that were extremely difficult to reach. In this regard, all credit is due to the honorable Mr. Wells, who describes so well the sufferings to be endured by anyone daring to venture into the fertile lands of the Valley of the Fallen. If the dangers of access were many, they were well repaid by the fecundity of its soil. Wells's writing has a singular beauty and there would be little merit in trying to emulate it, so I will instead transcribe, for the benefit of the reader, the entire passage in question: "The valley, he said, had in it all that the heart of man could desire—sweet water, pasture, a good climate, slopes of rich brown soil with tangles of a shrub that bore an excellent fruit, and on one side great hanging forests of pine that held the avalanches high. Far overhead, on three sides, vast cliffs of grey-green rock were capped by cliffs of ice; but the glacier stream came not to them, but flowed away by the farther slopes, and only now and then huge ice masses fell on the valley side. In this valley it neither rained nor snowed, but the abundant springs gave a rich green pasture, that irrigation would spread over all the valley space."

The next traces we find, closer to us in time than the era of Sancho Hacho, date from the eighteenth century and are related to the indigenous uprisings of San Miguel de Molleambato in 1766, provoked by the ruinous taxes imposed by the Marqués of Miraflores; and of San Phelipe in 1777, provoked by the Corregidor of Latacunga's insistence on undertaking a census of the natives. For centuries, it appears, the descendants of the men and women who had made their way along unknown paths to this valley in the shadow of the Cotopaxi volcano had lived a peaceful and isolated life, until one or the other of those eighteenth-century events led fifteen Spanish officers to flee from the fury of Indian rebels pursuing them with spears and shovels—and they fell into what may have been this same abyss. I found that information in a chronicle hidden within the pages of an agricultural manual that came by a circuitous path into the municipal archives of the city of Riobamba, though the report does not make clear whether this occurred before or after the volcano's minor eruption of 1766 or its major one in 1768.

What happened over the next hundred years is summarized in a few brief lines by Wells: "A strange disease had come upon them and had made all the children born to them there—and, indeed, several older children also—blind. And amidst the little population of that now isolated and forgotten valley the disease ran its course. The old became groping, the young saw but dimly, and the children that were born to them never saw at all." It is well known, from contemporary chronicles, that eruptions of the eighteenth century brought temporary blindness to nearby inhabitants and made it impossible, as far away as Quito, to see one's hand in front of one's face. Could this be cause of the initial blindness later prolonged by the genetic deterioration of the Valley's inbred population? Let us assume that Wells found the village in 1880. As I write these words in 1950, based on my recent research, I think that sometime after his visit the last descendants of that ancient pseudo-civilization based on what he called "the rudiments of a lost philosophy, the tradition of the greater world they came from, converted into something mythical and uncertain" must have finally left their valley for fear of another eruption that would sweep them from the earth, or perhaps because of other fears still unknown, and made their way to Guayaquil. I write these notes after having spent some weeks in that major port, pursuing certain clues to the south of the city on the banks of the salt-water estuary. Any information about this group of human beings that could be useful to men engaged in scientific endeavor would be welcome. My contact information will remain in the possession of the editors of this distinguished newspaper, the paragon of the national press. —Niall Binns

That was all. Varas continued searching in the papers of the time, but there was no response to this article-letter, nor any sequel to it. Binns disappeared, but that did not close the door that his article on the blind men had opened. For Varas, it was impossible to think that the figures who carried off the man on the stage were unrelated to those mentioned in the writings of Binns and Wells. But that left a lot of holes to fill. What happened between 1880 and 1950? What happened between then and 2006?

The Hole

Two weeks had passed.

"Where are you taking me? Who are you? What are you doing? Stop that!" The chubby man tried to get loose, waving his arms and kicking at the air, but it was no use.

He was surrounded by a group forming a tight circle around him. Two of them, inside the circle, had him by the armpits. They were all crowding him so closely that he barely had room to breathe. The little air there was reeked with a sickening odor of decomposition, rotting soil, worms. At some point he lost consciousness, and when he awoke he was sorry to have done so. He was being carried through a tunnel in the near-dark. The tunnel was so narrow that his captors had to go single file; they had him stretched out flat and were carrying him low down, near the floor, but when they noticed he had awoken they pushed at him until he understood he was supposed to stand and walk.

"Where are you taking me? What is this? I'm claustrophobic. Let me out of here!" His voice had gone reedy and weak. Earlier, when he'd tried to cry out, before he fainted, the walls had closed in on him so that his shouts echoed into what felt like infinity. He felt a sense of panic and a strong desire for a snort of cocaine to help him handle what was happening to him without losing control. These sons of bitches were going to give him a heart attack. He felt the blood pounding in his ears.

"Speak! Say something! What do you want from me? How much?" His voice quavered on the edge of hysteria.

The only answer was the sound of feet shuffling through a tunnel of dirt and silence.

✧ ✧ ✧

The residents of Poso Wells Cooperative were sick of soldiers. All those uniforms were making life impossible. Search after search, house after house, and every day they razed at least one. They closed four shops that served as unlicensed bars. They confiscated cans of black powder from a clandestine fireworks factory and arrested more than fifteen men for lack of papers and three women for leaving their small children locked in their shacks during the day while they went out to work. The people couldn't bear any more. How could the soldiers demand papers in good order when there wasn't even water to drink? Give them just that, just water, and they'd be first in line to play by the rules! A meeting was called in the plaza where the kidnapped man had disappeared.

"We have to do something right now, or they'll haul us all to jail," said a solidly built man of medium height, hoarse and sweating heavily.

"We need to take advantage of the fact that we're all

over the TV, demand deeds to our land, and get ourselves legalized once and for all," a woman answered him.

The woman was short and very attractive. She wore no makeup and let her hair fall loosely. A large lock fell over the middle of her face. In the afternoon breeze, her dress pressed against the smooth curves of her body, but these ceased to be the center of attention when, with a shake of her head, she revealed the scar that slanted from the outside of her right eye down into her cheek.

"No, we're not going to do any such thing, Bella, because I'm the one who solves the legal problems around here," the stocky man said. "And this is not the time."

"It's never the time," the woman answered him.

"What we're going to do is cooperate with the searches. We're going to help them so that they'll leave us be," the man went on, ignoring the last comment. He had a pistol poorly hidden beneath his shirt. "You're such a pain, you know that? Are you ever going to give up spouting opinions on everything? Somebody needs to give you a good working over. You need to be taught some manners, know what I mean?"

Now it was the woman's turn to ignore his comments.

"And you, are you ever going to stop speaking for us?" she retorted instead. "Things were already bad enough before the soldiers arrived." A murmur of approval and the sound of fans being flicked back and forth accompanied her words. "Maybe you don't know that, because you have a house here but you never sleep in it." She gave him a hard stare. "Or am I wrong?"

The atmosphere shifted as if a truck full of ice had passed through the middle of the plaza and charged the air with a blast of cold.

"We can demand street lighting, we've got a good reason for that now. They never would have snatched the man if there had been lampposts in the streets," the woman continued.

While Bella spoke, the man made his way through the river of people gathered in the dusk, until he was face to face with her.

"Didn't you hear me? We are not going to do *any* of that." He pronounced the *any* like a newly sharpened blade. "We're going to cooperate," he went on in a more light-hearted tone. "Without even being asked, because that's who we are, we are cooperators."

"Don't think I'm afraid of you, Don Chicho Salém. I've got enough experience with your goons. But some of us don't make our living through robbery or extortion"—here the crowd around her drew back—"and we know what kind of man you are. Don't count on me. I'm not going to be part of this."

The woman turned around and headed off into the streets through the gathering night. She walked without hurry and with her back erect. Before she disappeared from view, she heard a shot and then Salém's voice raised to a shout.

"Who else is leaving? Take note, ladies, that I'm not forcing anyone. Those who are with me, you're with me because you know what kind of man I am. Don't you come to me for help when you need it? Don't I lend you money when you ask? That woman is quite mistaken, and someday she'll realize her mistake. Probably too late. But, back to business. Who can I count on here?"

Several men raised their hands while some others took advantage of the commotion to slip away.

"Remember, I don't need you, I've got my own people. But don't think I won't collect payback for disrespect." Salém followed that up with a loud chuckle and another shot fired into the air, after which he grabbed his testicles in his meaty hands. "These are enough—and more—for me to do whatever I like, understood? Enough and more. Little prudes like Bella, they're afraid of the size of my treasure. That's why they run." His voice continued to echo through the empty streets.

Hearing him, Bella couldn't keep herself from saying aloud, "Ay, Don Chicho, aren't you old enough to know that it's not the size but what you can do with that thing?" At that moment she tripped on a rock. When she straightened up, she saw a dog sniffing at the dirt. Realizing there was an intruder on its street, the dog raised its head and looked her in the face.

"Your poor little prick, Salém, so pampered and innocent, while you're so guilty of having such a tiny brain and being satisfied with that. What you need is to stand in front of a mirror and repeat and repeat till you've learned the lesson: 'My little whistle isn't guilty of anything, it's no crime for it to be the way it is.' And when you've got that one down, you need to memorize another: 'I can stop being an idiot, I can learn not to be one.' With a little will power, anything is possible. Practice makes perfect, Don Chicho." All this, Bella said to the dog.

The animal ignored her speech, sticking its snout back into the hole in the bag of garbage it had found. Discovering a fish head, it caught the morsel in its teeth and took off down the street, wagging its tail with glee.

✧ ✧ ✧

Varas started to get pressure from the paper, demands to give them something: an article, a scoop, something to justify the pampered schoolboy's life they were subsidizing, so they said.

"I'm gathering facts," he said when he phoned his editor.

"Then give us some, because we need something. Congress is about to concede the election to the other candidate, and you spend two weeks scratching your balls, while we pay you to do it. Remember, Varitas, I'm not your rich uncle, and neither is the paper, do you hear me?"

"Go to hell, Eduardo. If I can confirm what I've got, you'll have the story of the year."

"Don't be funny, Varas. If you can manage to get the story, the attention span of our beloved public will be a day, at most. Remember, who wants yesterday's papers? What? You don't know the song, for Christ's sake? Yesterday's papers are good for wrapping fish guts in the market. I don't care about smoking guns or witnesses. I just want a story and I want it now!"

"And you'll have it, I swear, but you've got to give me more time. Understand? I need time, and you can shove the rich schoolboy's life up your ass. You're not giving me anything, so don't try to bullshit me. I help you make money and I'm only asking for a few more days to fill some holes. Even *First Impact* is going to want to buy this story from me. I haven't been sitting still, scratching my belly, like you." He heard a forced laugh from the other end of the line.

"Two days, Varitas. I'm giving you two days and then you can fuck off for real. Do you get that?"

"Yes, Señor Editor, I do."

✧ ✧ ✧

Varas left the house early in the morning, hardly even taking time for the cup of coffee Montenegro offered him. The old man always got up before the first rays of the sun appeared over the river. He liked that initial light of day, whose shimmering quality revealed only the outlines of things.

"Want to say where you're going so early?"

"Into shit, Don Montenegro, I'm going wading into shit."

Jaime Montenegro said nothing. The young fellow's tone of voice made it clear that he was nervous, and if what he really wanted was to wade into shit, he was in the right place, so let him go. The older man took his cup and sat by the rear window. The sunrise was beautiful, with fuchsia and violet sparkles flooding the sky. This was the only moment of the day when Montenegro felt life made any sense. Afterward, neon yellow made everything clear, and reality became obvious. Flat colors, all the same intensity, nowhere to lose oneself in silhouettes. That life didn't interest him.

Varas walked several blocks, followed by a substantial number of stray dogs. He stopped to buy bread from a store, and seeing how skinny the dogs were, he bought them some loaves too. He carried the bag to the vacant lot where it had all started and sat down on a mound of dirt to think. He started to eat the bread, still warm from the oven, and pulled off hunks to throw to the dogs. He entertained himself that way for a good while until, by chance, he threw a scrap that landed on top of the most distant of the mounds. One dog, the hungriest or most enthusiastic, it was hard to say which, went after it. Varas heard a loud *pum,* and then a moan. He got up and headed toward the sound. There was a hole, it looked like a small one, but as he pulled away rocks he could see it was wide enough for a grown man to fit through. Down below, the animal was still whimpering.

"Hang on, I'm coming to help you," he yelled into the hole.

However, Varas had the presence of mind to toss a small stone into the depths before descending. It seemed to fall forever until finally it hit bottom. He looked around and saw that the other dogs had left this one in the lurch, which reminded him of one of the first conversations he'd heard, in the barrio, about this vacant lot. He thought he should go down not only to help the dog but because this site right here, this hole, could be the clue he'd been looking for. But before finding out, he needed a flashlight and a rope.

"Listen, doggie, take it easy, I'm not going to leave you there. I'll be back," he called into the cavity before setting off down the unpaved street.

✧ ✧ ✧

Chicho Salém had organized his men and a few volunteers to search the barrio one house at a time. The idea was to find the missing man and turn him over to the authorities. Salém had a rough map of Poso Wells and gave his men orders to mark every house that had been searched with a coded sign. One of his men and one volunteer went on every search. There was a tacit agreement to let them in, as much to avoid problems with Salém as to get rid of the soldiers. Nobody wanted trouble with Don Chicho. There were too many rumors that no one needed to back up: That his prowess as a lawyer had more to do with physical force and arms than with eloquence before the bench; that he'd never lost a case; that all the judges and magistrates were on his payroll; that it didn't matter who was in power, because he always had the necessary contacts; that his influence extended from the coast to the mountains, where the drug trade, arms traffic, and money laundering made up still more of his many lucrative activities; and that activism on behalf of the poor in the southern reaches of Guayaquil was just another of his many masks. In spite of the fear sowed by all this, some people began to say that things were looking pretty slippery when they saw that the signs marking the searched houses were not all the same. But nobody offered explanations, and since so many foolish ideas circulated from mouth to mouth, in the end people decided to forget about it. Time passed, the searchers found nothing, the soldiers remained, and, to top it off, a crime wave had all the inhabitants of Wells on the edge of desperation. There was no police station in the barrio, and the majority of the victims would not go near one, anyway, to report the thefts of televisions, radios, and stereos. Nobody had seen anything. Nobody knew anything. Even a generator had disappeared. If you don't see anything, what can you say?

✧ ✧ ✧

Varas came back with a flashlight, thirty feet of rope, a hammer, a long metal pole, and a machete. There was no one around. A few blocks away, he could see the pack of dogs that had accompanied him in the morning. He got to work. First he hammered the pole into the ground, and when he was sure it was secure he tied one end of the rope to it with a series of sailor's knots, and the other end to his waist. He stuck the machete in his belt and the flashlight in his pocket. He lowered one leg into the hole, seeking support along the wall. Since the surface was not completely smooth, he was able to find some grooves to make use of. He brought his other leg inside and began the descent. Once he was completely inside, the stench nearly overpowered him: garbage, dampness, mold. He continued his descent and found the walls becoming softer and more porous. It was like sticking his hands into flan. He slipped, and in a desperate effort to break his fall into emptiness, he clung to the wall and found it sticky. He discovered that this made the descent easy. He pressed with his shoulders, with his stomach, and kept going down. He couldn't imagine what type of material was making this possible but there was no way to find out. He'd never been anywhere so dark. Dark, dank, suffocating. When the rope began to stiffen and he still had not touched bottom, he thought of jumping, hoping the bottom was not very far. Or else, climbing back up. Before he had time to decide, his feet hit a flat surface. Once on solid ground, he managed to separate his arms from the wall. The right side of his face and the whole front of his body were covered in sticky slime. He was confused. The darkness had disoriented him, leaving him unsure where he was or in what kind of shape. When he settled down—for he felt great anxiety and a need, rather irrational, to get out of there as quickly as possible—he reached into his pocket for the flashlight. Even in its beam, he couldn't see much. He kept the light in his left hand and, semi-consciously, the machete in his right. He followed what seemed to be a tunnel, downhill.

"Doggie, doggie, where are you?" His words sounded outsized down here. "Psst, psst, hurry up, I don't think you want to stay here, do you?" He was talking mostly to himself as he made his way along the corridor.

After a few steps, the darkness began to do a job on his mind. It was like walking through a nightmare with his eyes open, and it brought back every fearsome dream he'd ever had. He not only saw but heard hundreds of rats come charging down the passage toward him, attacking, overwhelming him, knocking him down. Their teeth tore burning gashes in his skin, yet all the while—perceiving and smelling and seeing this—he continued down the corridor. He felt the ground under his feet sliding away, felt himself falling into an endless well. He felt he could not resist the vertigo of his fall, but still he went on as if none of this were real. At some point the narrow tunnel emptied into a much wider one. Varas stopped and shone the flashlight around him. He saw a few caverns, not very deep. He tried to breathe slowly to regain his control. He went on.

"Doggie, doggie, come on out, right now. This is getting serious."

He spoke just to calm himself, not even aware of what he said. But they were words, and the words sheltered him. His leg brushed against something that wasn't dirt, nor was it the slime of the walls. He lowered his beam of light and saw something long and covered with mud. He kicked it and heard it complain.

"Let's get out of here. Come on, right now," he said, nearly in a whisper.

He tried pushing the thing again, this time more

gently, but nothing happened. Then he squatted down and shined his light on the dirt. Something moved, something that looked like a tangle of hair. He didn't remember the dog being that hairy, he thought it was more of a mangy mutt, the kind with more skin than hair. He kept shining the light, thinking he recognized the protruding ribs. He was about to lower his hand to pat and reassure the animal, but something held him back, so he kept exploring its body with his light. And then, more from surprise than anything else, he let out a cry and dropped both light and machete. It was an unconscious reaction for which he was instantly sorry. He reached out to grab the light and shine it on the shape once more. This time he met the gaze of the woman below him, who seemed barely aware of his presence. Right after that, he felt a tongue licking his face.

The Scar

Bella Altamirano entered the shop called El Descanso, owned by Rosa Quintero, her best friend. She greeted Rosa with a kiss that the shopkeeper returned automatically while wrapping up some herbs in newspaper and counting out the money a young girl was paying for them. Before putting the coins in her till, she lifted her head and offered Bella a smile. Inside the small windowless room, the air always smelled like diesel and carried the hum—more of a fly-buzz really —of the small generator that powered the refrigerator and a single low-wattage bulb hanging from the ceiling. When Bella came in, Rosa was behind the worn counter of her store—a plank of battered plywood placed across cases displaying all of her merchandise, clean and orderly, protected by translucent glass stained by dozens of fingerprints.

Bella did not return the smile. She asked for some oatmeal and a can of powdered milk.

"What's eating you?" her friend asked.

"Nothing, just that I used up all my Quaker and I

need some more to make soup." As she spoke, she opened a straw bag for Rosa to place her requests.

"Listen, sister, haven't I know you since we were six years old?" Rosa put the groceries into the bag and noted them in a ledger that included Bella's tab.

"No, don't write it down, I'm going to pay cash."

"Now you've really got me worried. You're hiding something, but it's louder than a donkey braying in a canyon."

"It's nothing," Bella said, eyes glued to the floor.

"Your scar is turning purple," Rose replied gently.

Bella smiled thinly, put the bag on the floor, and leaned toward Rosa.

"Can you believe I forget it's there?" she said while trying to see it out of the corner of her eye. As she did so, the scar lost the color Rosa had described.

Rosa rested her forearm on the counter, leaning toward Bella too.

"Is it Salém?" Rosa lowered her voice still further. "Do you think he might do something to you? Disappear you like the other women?"

"No, Rosa, Salém has been making threats for years, you know that better than anyone, but he's not going to dare touch me. One of his disguises is that he's a protector of women. How can he attack me or, worse, make me disappear? No, the disappearances aren't his work."

"What makes you so sure?"

"Because women are one of his best businesses, and if there's one thing Salém knows how to do it's bet on the winning horse. Does he help mistreated women out of Christian charity? Go check out his foundation's books. If he takes care of you, he collects from you too."

"Well, calm down little sister. It's one thing to clear the first hurdle and another to finish the race."

The two women grew quiet. During the silent interval accompanied only by the buzz of the generator, Rosa opened the refrigerator and took out two orange sodas. She uncapped them and started to drink from one while offering the other to her friend. The thin film of frost disappeared as soon as the bottles came in contact with the muggy atmosphere of the store. In the shadowy room, with her friend at her side, Bella recovered some of her ease and the illusion that everything could be as it had been before. But it was just an imperfect remnant, really, moments like this one in which she managed to forget about her scar. She had learned it was not necessary to disguise it with mother-of-pearl creams or musk rose oils, which in any case didn't work as advertised, nor to try to cover it up with endless layers of makeup, which didn't hide it but did stain her clothes. Nor did she part her hair to one side or straighten it to drop like a waterfall over her cheek. Well, sometimes out of habit she did the latter, but it was no longer from some tyrannical sense of duty to try to be the person she remembered. The wound, which had turned pink on scarring over, was the mark left by the only romantic relationship Bella was known to have had. The scar seemed to lead its own life: sometimes it was like the trace left by a crab on the seashore, but when she was angry it widened and turned a shade of violet. Then her face was like that of a broken and poorly mended doll. It was impossible to look at her without staring at the wound.

There were very few who would dare to ask her how she got the scar on her cheek, because the stories of its origin that circulated had cemented the fear and respect

Bella commanded in Poso Wells. Still, some truth could be sifted from the overlaps in the various versions one heard, which said that when Bella met Oswaldo Yerovi at the age of seventeen, she thought that life in this violent place was not only possible but maybe worth living. Then, after some years of peaceful cohabitation, not without joy and the birth of two children, her partner began to turn moody, to flare up without anything to justify his behavior. That was when Yerovi was said to have met Chicho Salém, who brought the young man to work with him at Bastión Popular, where Yerovi was also said to have a second family and home. Bella didn't trust the rumor mill. For her, seeing was believing, so one day she left her children with a cousin and shadowed Yerovi for twenty-four hours. That was enough. First, in the morning, she followed him to a clearing where, hidden from view by the bodies of some stripped cars, she managed to get close to the group of men who greeted her mate and, confident they could not be overheard, discussed their plans for the coming night. On the ground, spread on a dirty red cloth, she could see wallets, credit cards, cellphones, watches, and jewelry. Since the men took no care to lower their voices, she could hear all they said while drinking from a bottle that went from hand to hand.

"When those sonsofbitches are hung over, it doesn't even take any force," one said.

"Like taking candy from a baby," the one alongside him agreed.

"Old Salém opened the doors of paradise."

"Home of the goose that lays the golden eggs." Bella could see four gold teeth when this man smiled.

She went on listening behind the carcasses of stripped

automobiles for a good while, but nothing got any more specific and her husband didn't say anything, only drank one beer after another while sitting in a chair outside the main circle formed by the other men.

"So, everybody meet here at 11:30. Yerovi, don't forget your piece, now that you've got enough to buy one. If you don't bring it, don't get on the truck, because where we found you, we can find a hundred more. And be ready for anything. This is for real men. Remember, once you show what you're made of, Salém will start to think more of you."

Yerovi nodded but still didn't say anything. He emptied the bottle in his hand and then stood up and left. Bella didn't want to follow him through an unknown neighborhood so she decided instead, knowing what she now knew, to take advantage of a relative who used his car as a taxi at night. They agreed to meet around eleven at an intersection not far from the lot where she'd overheard Yerovi and the others. What Bella saw that night shattered her life. She would never forget the snickers of her husband and the rest of them, could never wipe out the vision of the flock of vultures gliding over the city, widening their circle and then diving to grab their prey. At about five a.m., after she'd seen them carry out robberies in several parts of town, the pickup in which her husband was riding slowed and then came to a stop. Bella could see three bodies on the ground: two men and a woman, all without helmets, who'd been thrown from a motorcycle and landed some yards in the distance. They looked like marionettes tossed at random: legs and arms at strange angles, the girl's hips out of line with her torso. All three were bleeding, their faces distorted with pain. The accident must have just happened, minutes before. When the seven men sprang from the bed of the truck, they took whatever they could find: phones, jackets, shoes, and watches. They didn't hesitate to lift up the bodies in search of wallets, as if these were not people but sacks of potatoes. Bella was surprised not only by their voracity but by the methodical way they went about their search. Her man's skill at this task made her nauseous, but she held on. The group abandoned the two men and concentrated their attention on the woman, beginning to strip her. They pulled at her pants, but her crumpled bones complicated the operation. Now they had ripped open her blouse, and her breasts, covered in blood and road grit, were exposed to the night, looking like freshly butchered meat. Bella began pounding desperately on the horn of the taxi, interrupting the group's laughter, until the driver grabbed her by the shoulders and slapped her.

"Are you trying to get us killed? Cut it out! Are you crazy?"

He grabbed her hands next, trying to stop her, but Bella kept flailing and repeating her blasts on the horn. Lights began going on in houses up and down the street. Her cousin drove off and, in the rearview mirror, Bella could see that the pickup was following them.

"Duck down. I'm going to try to get away from those bastards. If they catch us, we're dead."

This time Bella did as her cousin said, while he made sudden turns for what seemed like hours. Finally, on a busy street, she got out and took a bus. When she reached Wells, Yerovi still hadn't arrived. Midway through the morning, he showed up drunk. The children were already at school, and Bella had all his things packed in a box that she'd tied with a rope. When he tripped on his way to the bed, he kicked at it.

"Bella, *preciosa*, take these off for me," he said, pointing to his shoes.

His words were slurred, but his tone was friendly. Bella was surprised by the tenderness in his request. That friendliness had disappeared from the house months ago.

"Oswaldo, there are two ways to do this." She took a breath and held her voice steady. "You can go peacefully, or things can get violent, but one way or the other you're leaving."

"What?" Yerovi said, while trying to get comfortable on the bed and looking at her through unfocused eyes.

"You're going, I said."

"Where? What are you talking about? I'm tired, let me sleep."

"A lot of work?"

"Yeah, a lot. But—" he reached out his arm. "We haven't been together for a long time, have we? C'mere." His hand fell. "Bella, come on, take off your clothes."

The woman did not manage to get to the outhouse. Her body bent in two in the yard, vomiting up everything in her stomach. She splashed water on her face from a basin and went back in the house. Yerovi was snoring on the bed. A ray of sunshine fell like a whip across his face. Bella went to the kitchen and found a long carving knife that she stuck in her waistband. The bedroom reeked of aguardiente. She came to the bed and felt in the man's pockets and the folds of his clothes. No pistol. She got a glass of water and threw it on his face.

He sat up, shocked and angry.

"Are you nuts? What the fuck are you doing?"

His eyes were red. He kept on shouting, rubbing his eyes, and shaking his head from side to side.

"I told you, you're leaving." Bella pointed at the box on the floor. "There's your stuff."

Yerovi stood up and walked toward Bella. Passing the window, he saw a group of women outside, looking his way.

"Fucking vultures! Get out of here. You want something to gossip about? Is that what you want?" He stuck half his body out the window while screaming like he'd gone crazy himself. Then he turned around and headed back toward Bella, who hadn't moved or said another word.

"That's what it's about? Those busybodies came flocking around with the story that I've got another woman? Who are you going to believe, them or me?"

Bella still kept quiet. Yerovi sat down and put his head between his hands, elbows resting on the table they used for meals. He seemed to have forgotten about her. When he looked up, his voice had changed.

"Bella, we're getting out of here. I can't stand this place." He looked at her with tears in his eyes. "We can't go on this way. We can't do anything, we can't even screw without everybody knowing, it's like living with our insides hanging out. I'm not an animal."

"Really?" Bella felt she was collapsing, she wanted to hug her husband, to tell him it had all been a bad dream, but then she remembered the girl. "How long did you think it would take me to find out?"

"It's nothing, Bella. You're my wife. I'll get rid of her tomorrow morning, first thing, but listen to me, let's get out of here."

"What are you talking about?" she asked.

Yerovi looked at her differently. He stood up, came over to her, took her by the shoulders.

"What are you talking about?"

"I'm not talking about any woman, Oswaldo. Last night I followed you—" she looked him in the eyes. "I followed you all night long, and I want you to leave this house and never come back."

This is the point where things get confused. Some people say that Bella, before he could react, pulled the knife from her waistband and, closing her eyes to find the courage to use it, cut off one of his ears and blinded him in the left eye.

Others say that Yerovi grabbed a bottle from the table where he'd been resting his elbows minutes before. He smashed it to so as to have a weapon to kill his wife to keep her from going to the police about what she had seen, and it was then, before Bella could get the knife out in front of her, that he sank the sharp edge of the broken bottle in her cheek and left her branded with the mark.

Facts. The truth is always somewhere above, below, or next to the facts. The truth is that only when the light was dim, or in the shadows of a darkened room, or just at dawn when everything still appeared in silhouette, did Bella continue to be beautiful in fact as well as in name. That was the only truth.

Waiting Forever for You

That was certainly not what he'd been expecting to find when he went down the hole in search of the dog. *Now what kind of mess have I gotten myself into?*, Varas asked while he carried the woman through the gloomy tunnel in search of the way out. He knew he had followed a straight line, with no forks that he could remember, never choosing between one branch or another as best he could recall. But now he couldn't find the shaft of light that ought to pierce the ceiling somewhere, nor the rope that should be hanging from the world outside. Either he'd lost all sense of time or he'd been here many more hours than he thought, or else reality, down in this place, stretched itself out into something very different. He stopped and lowered the woman to the ground, then leaned against the wall and let himself slide down too. He had forgotten the slimy texture, in no way reassuring, but at this point what did he care? What he needed to do was think. The dog, which had been following him, covering his rearguard, came up to him and resumed its licking. The animal's warm breath in the stifling atmosphere of the tunnel didn't bother Varas. In fact, it comforted him.

"Cuauhtémoc," he said, scratching the dog's head. "That's your name, after the eleventh Aztec emperor. That guy had balls. There was Cortés torturing him to get him to reveal where the gold was hidden, and there was Cuauhtémoc, my buddy Témoc, calmly keeping it together while they burned the soles of his feet." Varas stopped talking, but kept stroking the animal's back, and after a moment he laughed. "He must have felt like a fallen eagle, and here we are, you and me, as fallen as can be." When he said that, some mechanism clicked back into action. He stood up and, without any transition, went on, "But not totally lost, are we, Temocsito? Look, you go in front this time and I'll follow you, because that's what friends are for. You game?"

With the animal as his guide, Varas concentrated on following, which allowed him to discard all the ideas that had accompanied him since he found the naked, mud-caked woman in the tunnel: that he'd fallen through a wrinkle in time, that on dropping into the hole his reality had lost its footing and logic had lost its hold. Because, after all, why would a woman be crawling and grunting, unable to speak, in a tunnel closed in by scum-covered walls? Better not think about it. If he could get out, then there'd be time to find some kind of answer. Témoc started barking, the sound bouncing down the tunnel, echoes of echoes until the echoes revealed the rope, still in place. When Varas managed to see it, in the faint light from the fading flashlight, his face lit up. At last they had a way out, but how? The woman could not climb by herself, and he didn't know how he could scale the gummy wall that would swallow his foot if he tried to put any weight on it. And Témoc?

✧ ✧ ✧

"These papers need to be signed," said the sickly-looking man wearing a sea-blue suit and sky-blue silk shirt, maintaining his posture by the window. The two men were in the huge conference room of the Vinueza Consortium, located on the fourteenth floor of the only building in Ecuador with artificial intelligence, near the Colón Hilton in Guayaquil. Once an entrant presented badges and magnetic cards to clear security, the building—one more employee of the company—took charge of offering services. There were no buttons in the elevators, because the building recognized the voices of those who entered and deposited them at their desired floors. It maintained an ideal temperature, purified the air with constant shots of ozone into the ventilation system, opened doors, and projected statistics and sales charts in the air thanks to a sophisticated program that gave such abstractions three-dimensional form. Cutting-edge technology, available only on the top three floors occupied by the officers of the firm, allowed holograms to display the human body, specifically that of the female, in the most varied positions. The two men were conferring at an oak table, several yards long and oval in shape, in the center of the room. Fourteen red leather armchairs lent the space an austere grandeur.

"José María, signed by whom?" replied the other, a graying man of more than sixty-five, his blurry right eye blinking constantly. Close up, the thick cataract was quite visible.

"What do you suggest, Pablo? That we stand here with our arms folded while one of the Corporation's most lucrative deals slips away?" responded José María, a short man whose sickly appearance was complemented by a prominent belly that suggested he hadn't offered his soft body even a single day of exercise in all his forty-five years. He was pale, and his skin was covered with a fine layer of cold sweat that made him look like a fish. "We can change the date and forge his signature," he concluded.

"I didn't hear that." The older man stood and walked over to the window. Then, more quietly, he modified his statement. "You didn't say that."

He went on looking out the window and then turned around to face José María. "I don't need to remind you that you have no say over what happens in the Corporation. Correct me if I'm wrong, but you're the administrative director of the Vinueza Enterprise Group. It's Andrés's brother who's in charge of the Corporation."

"If it makes you more comfortable, fine, I didn't say it," José María answered. After another pause, he continued. "Tell me, since when has Andrés's brother taken charge of anything? And where do I find him so he can sign the documents? Who do you think you're talking to, Pablo? Andrés has—or I should say 'had'—power of attorney to handle everything." Closing his eyes till they seemed two horizontal lines, he looked less like a slippery fish, and more like an eel with an upset stomach.

"No notary will certify that document. Everybody's talking about his disappearance," Pablo continued.

José María smiled. Pablo, the most senior partner, the only one remaining from the era in which Vinueza Jr.'s father had personally seen to all the business of all ninety companies, had already implicitly given him carte blanche. As long as Pablo didn't have to know about it, José María could do whatever he thought necessary. That role didn't bother him. With the results quantified in millions, his scruples could stay packed away forever in a box. But his smile also reflected Pablo's failure to object to his use of the past tense. If all else failed, that was the next step, Plan B: get a judge to declare Andrés Vinueza legally dead. But as of yet, there was no need for things to go that far. Not with the photos José María had in his possession.

✧ ✧ ✧

Varas had always defended his comic books against his mother's ill-intentioned attacks. To his mother, reading comics meant, automatically, being lazy and good for nothing. He'd managed to make a deal with her, that if his grades stayed high, there was no god who could take his comics away. Also, once he was old enough to have a job, he earned his own money to buy them. His tastes inclined toward anything created by Stan Lee, the sage of Marvel Comics. But not even when he was reading them so avidly in his adolescence could he have imagined how useful the comics would turn out to be. Thinking about how to get out of the tunnel with the woman and the dog, he pressed his hands against the wall and, in the darkness, what came to him was the first issue of *Spiderman*, the one where Peter Parker discovers that his wrists emit a thick, sticky substance that must have been much like what Varas was touching now. Thanks to the substance, Spiderman could climb walls. Varas gave it a try. His stretched out his arms and pushed first his right foot and then his left against the tunnel wall. He began climbing slowly. When he found that this really did work, he climbed back down. Once on the ground he considered how to carry the woman, because that was what he had to do. She had neither the will power nor the strength to hang from his neck. The only option that occurred to him was to place her in front of him and tie her to his body with the rope, making her into an extension of himself while he climbed toward the world outside. The tension that had focused all his attention on getting out of there had obscured the fact she was naked, which now made him most uncomfortable. This was neither the time nor the place to feel what he was feeling, but there it was, out of his control. He took off his shirt and covered her with it. Temóc rubbed against his leg and Varas pushed him away, now in a bad mood. A question began to flutter in his brain: *What lie am I telling myself?* He decided to leave that unanswered. He wrapped the shirt around the woman, pressed her against his body, and tied the rope. He performed his Spiderman feat and reached the surface sooner than he expected. There was no one around. Judging by the position of the sun, it was about noon. He leaned the woman against one of the mounds of dirt and told her he'd be right back. Then, before descending, he adjusted some long locks of her mud-caked hair to cover her face. If the intensity of light beaming down from the sky was making his eyes burn, he could only imagine what it was doing to hers. While he looked at her he wondered again what she could have been doing in the tunnel, but none of the answers that shuffled through his brain made sense. Some hidden truth was eluding him. By the time he had lowered himself halfway back into the hole, he was feeling trapped between two worlds: the world of light and that of shadows. He decided that no truth he was going to find would be sufficient to explain her. Or anything else.

✧ ✧ ✧

"Listen, if they indict me for doing what you want, I'll lose my license." The man paced back and forth while he rubbed his sweaty hands. "Do you know what that means?"

"What I know, Fernández, is that you owe your personal fortune entirely to Vinueza Enterprises . . ."

"Legally acquired, my dear José María, a fortune legally acquired, the fruit of fulfilling the duties of my profession," the man interrupted, staring fixedly at José María, who sat comfortably in front of an enormous window overlooking the city's waterfront promenade.

"And you bought this office with the proceeds from your contract to notarize all the real estate transactions for the city's urban renewal program. Do you remember who got you that contract?" While José María spoke, his skin acquired its characteristic aquatic luminosity. "Along with all of Salém's contracts for legalizing the squatter settlement land. And when Andrés's father decided to change his will, you were the one to rewrite it for him. Remember what happened with that inheritance, Fernández?"

"I acted strictly in accordance with the law, José María. You know very well what a notary does in this country: he advises both parties in relation to any issue that requires a legal opinion on a contract or other action submitted for his consideration."

"I studied law too, Fernández, and in my case I passed the exams. We have notaries in order to avoid disputes, so the courts don't get clogged with too many lawsuits. A

59

notary's work is above all preventive, as in the case of wills, which he drafts so as to avoid future legal conflicts after the death of the testator. Remind me, Fernández. Has it been nine years or ten?"

"Since what?" The man was nervous but also angry, barely containing the annoyance in his voice.

"Since the trials, Fernández, the trials," José María answered him calmly.

"Which ones? Whose?" The notary's voice had risen in pitch.

"About the will. You're not going to tell me you've forgotten Señor Vinueza's will?"

"What does that have to do with me?" the notary yelled.

"With you? I can't believe you're so incurious, given how involved you were in the process of writing the document. But who am I to try to plumb the depths of human behavior?" José María stood up and walked closer to the window, slowly, letting his last comment permeate the air in the office. "So far, the trial has been going on for ten years—actually, ten and a half. The document is so confusing, offers room for so much speculation and interpretation . . . sometimes one could doubt the competence of its author. The previous version, written by notary number twenty-nine, a friend of the deceased, was a paragon of clarity, but it was so ungenerous toward Andrés. Do you remember that, Fernández?"

"José María, I don't understand where you're taking this, but I can assure you that there's no way you can suggest I'm guilty of anything." Fernández had not moved from behind his enormous desk of polished lignum vitae. "Of anything at all."

"I think we're talking past each other, my dear José Manuel. What I came for was to ask you a favor. A favor for a mutual friend."

"And I've been telling you, for more than an hour, that I can't do anything. That my hands are tied by the law. That I have a high opinion of Vinueza Enterprises and its management, but there's nothing I can do."

"Is that your last word? Nothing can make you change your mind? Not even these photographs?" José María extended a handful of images toward the notary.

And he smiled.

✧ ✧ ✧

Varas picked the woman up and began to walk toward Montenegro's house. He had the rope wrapped around his chest, the machete stuck once again in his belt, behind him, and the flashlight and hammer in his pockets. Témoc followed. They descended the unpaved streets as if they were the only inhabitants of Poso Wells. Nobody saw them, nobody wanted to know. They were covered with mud and looked like phantoms. When they reached Montenegro's house, he opened the door for them.

"You're a mess, Gonzalo," the old man said, while gesturing for them to come in.

Varas smiled. "If you only knew, Don Montenegro, if you only knew." Varas and his entourage remained on the front stoop.

"What do I need to know, *muchacho*?" Montenegro turned abruptly, disappeared inside, and returned with something under his arm. "Aren't you coming in? What are you doing out there?"

He placed a plastic cover over the rattan sofa in the front room.

"Put the girl down here while you go wash your face."

"Can I use one of your bowls to put out water for the dog?" Varas asked from the kitchen.

"Sure, sure," Montenegro said.

Varas came back with a glass for the woman and put Témoc's bowl on the floor. When he tried to bring the glass to her lips, the woman seemed to see him for the first time. Something in her attitude had changed in the short interval. She stiffened her neck, raised her head, and sat up in the couch. Suddenly she didn't look like a terrified animal. She took the glass and drank without any help. It was just then, when Varas first saw her as a human being and not as a problem, that he fully realized how strange the situation was. She was covered in a thick layer of gray mud that had dried and was beginning to crack off against the plastic sheet. The dog was soiling the floor of the house with its dirty paws and back, and Varas had to be every bit the mess that Montenegro had implied. He looked at Montenegro again and opened his mouth.

"Gonzalo, wait, there's no hurry, you can explain it all later. In the back yard there's a barrel with water and there's soap, too, and you know where your towel is. Show the young lady where she can clean up"—a smile passed over his face—"and, by the way, why don't you do that too?"

The three went out into the yard. Varas offered a washcloth to the woman and showed her the bar of soap.

"I'll bring you some clothes, I'll be back," he told her, while he climbed the steps to the back door.

When he returned, the woman had removed the shirt he'd put on her and was throwing water on her naked body. Varas was mad at himself again. Though he wanted to keep watching her body appear from under the mud, he opted, against his will, to cough.

"I'm leaving you some pants and a shirt."

He climbed up the steps once more and, although he intended to step inside, he stayed there, like a peeping tom, unable to resist. When he came back down, she was drying her hair and still hadn't dressed. Varas began to throw water on Témoc and, when he finished and the woman showed no sign of leaving, he began to undress too. He had to turn his back while washing because his body was betraying him again. Témoc, meanwhile, never stopped wagging his tail while she rubbed the towel on his back and scratched him behind the ears. Varas thought that any observer would take them for a happy family. That showed what appearances were worth.

✧ ✧ ✧

"Does that offer you a different perspective?" José María said, continuing to smile and watching the notary's face as he studied the photos.

"All I can say is that you ought to hire a better photographer, because it's hard to make anything out," the notary answered.

"Tomorrow morning, some or all of these pictures could appear in the paper, sufficiently enlarged," José María responded in the same neutral tone as before.

"So?"

"José Manuel, I'm afraid we're still not communicating. Those are pictures of your son, he's naked in some rather compromising positions, and not exactly with a girl."

"That's what I'm saying, who would be interested in them?" The notary poured himself a glass of whiskey and raised the bottle toward José María. "I imagine you'd like a drink too?"

"I don't want to drink with you, and I don't have all day. To make things clear between us—and I'm only going to say this once—if you don't notarize all the documents I gave you with the new date, then these pictures and more like them will appear in every newspaper we have in this country. Do you understand?" Now the calm had vanished from his voice.

"The one who doesn't seem to understand is you, José María. That signature is false, we both know it, and I'm not going to risk my career for a document. And don't worry about the pictures, because nobody's family will go up in smoke if you publish them. I've known about it for years, my son and I had a long conversation, and the whole city knows his tastes. Where have you been hiding, José María? You work too much, you don't get out enough, you ought to take a vacation once in a while." He drank a long swallow of whiskey and swirled the ice in the glass, producing a delicate tinkling sound. "And if that's all, you know where the door is. I've got work to do."

VI

Órale Pinche Güey

As soon as he started up the stairs, Varas realized what had been nagging at him since he had rushed out of Poso Wells with the girl and the dog, jumping into the first taxi that was willing to pick them up. He had forgotten his keys, left them at Montenegro's. It didn't worry him that much, though, because a little shove was all it would take to force his feeble latch and most likely topple the door. When they got to the third floor, he could hear music coming down the stairwell. Their luck was beginning to change, he thought. At the fifth floor they left the stairs and made their way along a dim hallway partially lit by a small window revealing battered walls. By the time they reached the end, the music had grown deafening. Varas had barely touched the last door when it opened as if by a miracle. A man in his early thirties with wide sideburns and the aggressive appearance of an indie rocker stood in the doorway. His ravishing smile completely contradicted his avant-garde cynic's attire.

"*Carnal!*" the man shouted over the din.

"Turn down the fucking volume, *pinche güey,* or I'm

throwing you out even if you do live here," Varas responded with a big smile of his own.

"*Mamón!* Let me give you a hug." Benito del Pliego did not make the slightest move in the direction of the stereo.

"At least change the record, man. You know what your fucking favorite alternative rockers did after this album, don't you? They started singing covers of Julio Jaramillo, finally came to their *pinche* Mexican senses."

Benito remained standing there in the doorway as if he were talking to the postman, or so absorbed in the conversation that he failed to realize Varas was waiting in his own doorway to come in. "And loyalty?" he demanded. "And my obsessions, *güey*? What about them? They must count for something. And don't start in on my homeboys. When you pick a fight about Café Tacuba, that argument never ends well."

"No argument, *ñañito*," Varas said, reaching for the best Quichua term of affection and resisting the trendy temptation to attempt to sound more *mexicano* than thou. "I'm tired, brother. All I want is a cold beer." As he said that, his shoulders sagged. In front of his friend, he could reveal just how vulnerable he felt.

"Sure, sure, but what else do you expect?" Benito continued. He stepped back at last, allowing Varas's living room to come into view: a collapsing couch, two wooden chairs with caned seats, piles of books, a barely functioning stereo—decibel level excepted—with a halfway broken CD player and a cassette player in equally bad shape. An old black-and-white TV completed the furnishings, along with two big planters, one holding a fern and the other a croton, both looking healthy and leafy under a picture window. "I mean, I'm a *defectuoso* from the D.F., Mexico City in my blood."

"The hell you are, *mi poeta*. What about your Spanish grandfather, your father from Veracruz, and mother from Manabí? You've got about as much Distrito Federal in your genes as I do." Varas stepped in, took a quick look around, and added, "Thanks for watering the plants, man. Now if you'll just do the same for me and my friends"—he turned off the music and pointed toward the door—"you don't know how many points you'll have scored with St. Peter when the moment comes."

The poet turned around and caught sight of the dog and the barefoot woman for the first time.

"Let me introduce the mysterious damsel in distress, who very soon, I'm sure, will tell us her name and where she came from," Varas said, dropping into one of the empty chairs. "And Témoc, the boldest and most loyal of mongrels, named in honor of your national hero number one."

Once introduced, Témoc entered as if he'd always lived there. He hopped onto the couch, where he lay down on a pile of papers that had fallen in a corner. The poet followed him. "Órale, your *pinche* Témoc is making himself comfortable on my poems." He pulled the papers out from under the animal, which didn't disturb it at all.

Varas stood up, took the pages from Benito, and read aloud:

Surprise is taken for granted in a world turned routine
Making a party out of a workday dyes your pages red.

"Our Temocsito is absolutely fearless," he remarked, "but as for a literary critic, I don't know. When did you write this?" The smile never leaving his lips, he added, "Sorry I left you alone for so long, *pinche güey.*"

The poet barely heard his friend because he hadn't taken his eyes off the woman. She had something he'd seen in very few attractive women, in that she didn't notice the effect she had on men, or rather, she didn't care. She said nothing, her face gave nothing away, and that vacuum made her irresistible because it allowed you to imagine anything. The poet was starting to like her. No better way to fall in love than with a completely blank slate.

"Now I get why you've been gone so long, *hermanito.* Come in," he urged the woman. "Come in."

But the silence was enough to suggest to the poet that the situation was less obvious than it seemed and he should make himself scarce while things took their course. There was nothing to drink in the apartment, and Varas had been gone for nearly a month. Benito went to the store for beer, skipping happily down the stairs while humming his favorite Café Tacuba anthem, the one Varas hated most.

Ya chole chango chilango
Que chafa chamba te chutas
no checa andar de tacuche
y chale con la charola.

How many times had he argued that it didn't matter if this was a song no one born outside of Mexico City could understand, let alone those born outside the country whose capital it was? How many times had he explained that three quarters of the globe spoke languages neither he nor Varas could comprehend, and this didn't keep the world from turning, so who cared? What difference did it make if you couldn't get half the lyrics as long as the song sounded good and meant something to someone? Words, what the fuck were they? The two of them both spoke Spanish and they still could barely communicate, which didn't keep them from being soul brothers, *carnales de alma*, after all. But when he hiked back up the stairs with six cold liter bottles of beer, a gallon of water, a box of coconut cookies, three bars of Manichos and some bones for the dog, he allowed himself to hum a different tune.

"Valentina, Valentina, I surrender to all of your charms. / If they're coming for me tomorrow, let them kill me right now in your arms." This was the best song he knew for keeping the grim reaper at bay, so it wouldn't hurt to sing it just in case. Because the woman and the dog smelled more like trouble than like an attempt at family life on the part of his friend. Though he hoped—truly—that he was wrong.

When he opened the door, the stereo was offering up Julio Jaramillo, a *pasillo* tragic as the best, yet cheerful too. Maybe there really was something to celebrate. No one but Témoc was in the living room. Del Pliego could hear the shower going, and the bedroom door was closed.

"Maybe you'd care to explain all this to me?" he said to the dog. He walked toward the kitchen while the Ecuadorian Nightingale crooned, "I'm in a world of troubles and shipwrecked by love in the void. . . ."

"*Pinche* romantic *mamón*," Benito declared, and he disappeared behind the other bedroom door.

VII
A Mass for the Dead

It was a small chapel that had seen better days. The streets of the Barrio del Centenario were barely lit at night, and from the flowerbeds in front of the church grew weeds that sought footholds in the wall. Missing paving stones gave the sidewalk the appearance of an old man's mouth with missing teeth, while rodents scurried in and out of these gaps, day and night. To José María, all this made it the ideal spot. He paid the local priest the small sum previously agreed upon for renting the chapel, without specifying why he needed it. He added a few bills to suggest that if the priest asked no questions, he would tell him no lies. What he had forgotten to consider was that the local residents might begin speculating about the cause of the break in the usual routine. He'd bought silence within the church, but hadn't made any agreement with those outside. When they saw the enormous gilded candelabras, the bouquets of flowers and then the coffin being unloaded from the truck, the locals began asking questions and, when they got no answers, inventing their own. The truck bore the logo of Empresas Vinueza, and soon someone put

71

forward the hypothesis that this was to be the scene of a wake for the man who had disappeared, the renowned businessman Andrés Vinueza, and that rumor soon spread throughout the southern reaches of the city. When José María arrived at noon, he was in a very bad mood. He had more important things to do, he thought, than spend hours in clogged streets traversing the city from north to south. His mood grew still worse when he was greeted by a bevy of television cameras at the chapel door. As soon as he got out of the car, he saw the priest, surrounded by reporters, signaling him. He realized that things had taken an unexpected turn. How had anybody found out? And the press? None of this was in the script. Microphones were shoved in front of his face and questions came at him like machine gun fire.

"Who are you, sir? Whom are you representing?"

"Why wasn't Vinueza's wife named as his legal representative?"

"Has the body been found? The police haven't said so."

"Does this mean the presidential campaign is over, because there's no need for a run-off now?"

"According to Article 193 of the Civil Code, it takes ten years after a disappearance for an individual to be declared legally dead."

"Paragraph three of that same article defines disappearance by violent means and says in that case the delay is three months. Why is a mass being held when less than a month has gone by?"

"Is this being treated as a political kidnapping?"

José María's skin was now covered with a cold white substance that gave off an evil smell, his mouth frozen into a dead man's rictus. The reporters took a few steps back to get away from the odor but they kept up the barrage of questions. He hadn't answered any when a small woman, less than five feet in height, stepped forward and threw her arms around his waist. Her eyes were red, she was sobbing, and her mucus began to stain the white percale of his Galliano dress shirt. Under most circumstances he would have shoved her away, but at this point her interruption was more than welcome.

"Ay, Don José María, my baby Andrecito, why did this have to happen to him?" she whimpered.

Where did he know this woman from? He tried in vain to remember, all the while stroking her back in condolence while the cameras rolled.

"You're a true friend," she said through her sobs. "Not even his wife is here, but you are, you are. Oh my God, how can this be happening, but this is when we see who our true friends are."

That wrinkled face, those forearms shaking like jelly, that scent of fried fish and rancid, reheated oil—now he knew! This was the woman who raised Andrés, his nanny, who was still employed in the kitchen. He'd seen her gliding like a shadow through the hallways of the mansion when the Vinuezas were entertaining guests. How had she heard about the mass? Using her as a shield, he pushed through the crowd and into the church. He went over to the other priest, the one he'd hired to conduct the service, and told him to get started. When the clergyman stood in front of the altar there was sudden silence, though the cameras continued to flash like lightning that José María willed himself to ignore. He concentrated on summoning his best expression of suffering, a desolation beyond words.

"Oh Lord, we commend to you the soul of your

servant Andrés Vinueza, and we pray, Jesus Christ, Savior of the World, that you do not deny him entry into the lap of your patriarchs, for this is why you mercifully came from heaven unto earth."

A murmur of surprise and then of assent could be heard, followed finally by a few sobs.

"I told you it was for the guy who disappeared," one voice asserted.

"Who croaked," another voice corrected.

José María sank his head toward his chest and covered his forehead with one hand.

"Lord, fill his soul with joy at your presence and disregard his sins past or present, and the excesses to which heedlessness or lust may have led him."

✧ ✧ ✧

"Justice is beautiful in its symmetry."

"It is wise and cruel."

"Its law reigns by day and by night."

"It punishes the sinner."

"And rewards the just."

"The just are like trees planted beside flowing water."

"That give fruit in their season."

Day after day, a group of squatting men repeated this strange litany that was driving Andrés Vinueza out of his mind. For the first few weeks, he tried to interrupt with questions, since this was the only moment of the day when he had contact with anyone, but the kicks to the stomach he received in response soon dissuaded him from trying to find out anything. Nonetheless, as time went on and he grew more accustomed to the conditions in which he was living, he was able to tie together the few loose ends that his dulled senses managed to grab on to: There were five men in a circle (this he could conclude from the sound of their voices in the cavern). Sometimes they squatted, sometimes went down on their knees, though he'd never been able to glimpse the transition. They wore bells that produced a dull sound, bells that must be hanging from some part of their bodies and that allowed him to sense their comings and goings. The sound reminded him of Swiss cowbells. After considerable thought—because he had plenty of time to think—he concluded that this distinction must imply some rank in a hierarchy. There were other noises in the cavern that sounded like they were made by something that was crawling, and he was sure those must be human beings too. Or the approximation of humans who kept him trapped here underground, with god only knew how many tons of earth above his head. Although he could not see, he had felt every inch of the place where his kidnappers had put him and where it was impossible to stand up. The tunnel, the cavern, whatever it was, was less than a meter high in this part and had to be very far from the surface because of the bone-chilling cold. Whereas for the first few days he had been stifling hot, now he shivered and expected that a case of pneumonia would soon put an end to his suffering. No one had said a word about a ransom, and the only thing he knew for sure was that his captors spoke an archaically accented Spanish in deep and rasping voices. And that he was never going to see the light of day again.

✧ ✧ ✧

"Oh good Lord Jesus, we firmly believe that you, who pitied the pain of others throughout your life, will look with mercy on the souls of our loved ones in Purgatory. Oh Jesus, hear our prayer, and in your mercy grant to those whom you have taken from us the gift of eternal rest in the bosom of your infinite mercy and love. Grant them, Lord, eternal reward in the everlasting glow of your countenance."

The priest went to the niche that held the chalices and a small, egg-shaped urn with several chains attached to its upper half. When he opened it, smoke rose from inside and the small chapel filled with the scent of incense and aromatic wood. The priest pushed his way through the crowded chapel until he reached the coffin, where he began to swing the censer like a pendulum.

"Thou, beloved Father, pity our tears as well. Accept them, Lord, as the blood of the wounded soul, flowing for the loss of him who was your beloved servant, your loyal friend, and your faithful Christian."

Outside, a thunderclap of nearly cataclysmic proportions seemed to split the sky in two. The crowd, already filling the narrow limits of the chapel, found itself pushed forward by newcomers who, seeing the open door, dashed in to escape the sudden downpour and then, curiosity aroused, tried to get closer to the altar to see what was going on. The priest, unaware, continued with the service.

"Behold our tears, Lord, the heartfelt tribute we offer for his soul, that you might purify it in your precious blood and raise it promptly to heaven, if it is not enjoying that rapture even now."

By now, it was becoming impossible to breathe. The priest, standing at the far end of the coffin, was waving the censer with heartfelt passion. Someone had closed the door in order to shut out the tropical cloudburst, but water flowed in underneath and the door began to shake like someone in the grip of an epileptic fit. The hinges popped. Those closest to the coffin were coughing with streaming eyes, while those behind them pushed forward to get away from the water, creating a moving wall with no defined shape but plenty of force, a wall that soon crashed into the priest, who fell onto the coffin and toppled it from the improvised base on which it had been resting. When it hit the floor, the poorly joined boards tore apart. The old woman seated at José María's side began to scream. The videographers who had turned off their cameras and the reporters who had stopped taking notes because they could barely breathe all sprang back into action. Just then, as someone opened the doors wide and water flooded in, soaking the attendees who were blinded by the camera lights and suffocating from the smoke, José María slipped away.

"My child, what have they done with my child! My God, what kind of monster would do this?" screamed the woman while she watched the fragments of the empty coffin being trampled by the people jammed inside the chapel.

José María drove off, proceeding with extreme caution through the whirling crosswinds that descended on the city. He was stuck in a line of traffic again, now moving toward the north. It occurred to him that he should have ordered a metal coffin, which would have survived the fall, but he didn't spend much time on that. He tried to dry his hair with his hands and, finding this impossible, gave up and pressed number seven on his sound system. Soon the voice of Ricardo Arjona had drowned out both the noise outside and that within José Maria's worried brain. He sang along with his favorite performer as if he had not a care in the world.

✧ ✧ ✧

"Thou camest and conjoined heaven and earth and thou hast broken the cycle of the snakes. Now is the hour to rise into the presence of the angels," said one of the voices.

"To tarry with the lizards in the world of the present. It is time, thou art the envoy, the promised one. All the signs have been given," continued another.

"So spoke the old ones, in truth, and in truth I say that thou wilt see the sky open and the angels of God rise and fall upon the Son of Man," the third intoned.

The man who had been sunk in the mud and his own excrement for—was it two weeks? three?—could not understand anything but he realized that this time they were speaking to him and doing so with deference, as if something had changed. The oldest, the fourth one with the broken voice, came closest to offering an explanation.

"In the beginning a void was opened in the rock and issued forth things inanimate, senseless, and flames, and other creatures with only the barest of intellect, and then came men and then at last the angels who can be heard singing and fluttering but whom no one can touch."

The words offered him no reassurance. Flames? Angels? He was surrounded by a band of madmen.

"Thou art the Envoy, he who will allow us to leave these walls that oppress us and to feel the air once more upon our heads," the fifth man uttered. "An enormous room where a hundred men, one atop the other, will not reach the roof of soft rock that protects us from the void."

Andrés Vinueza decided that this was not a moment to ask questions but rather to listen to what was being said. Soon he would escape from this gang of imbeciles who mixed biblical texts with the most esoteric beliefs. Lizards? Snakes? Celestial beings? Once they were outside, it would be a different story, but until then he was in their hands. As he listened, from some remote corner of his brain came the parable of Jacob's Ladder. What these brutes were saying reminded him of catechism classes. Did they take him for some minor Messiah? The incarnation of a deity? If so, why had they mistreated him so? Just before they left him, he heard —mixed with sound of their rattles— something that diverted him from those thoughts.

"Thou shalt provision us with women and we will be strong once more. Thou shalt see, we will protect thee, and thou too shalt prosper," proclaimed all five in a ragged, unsynchronized chorus that added a strange resonance to their words.

Women? Why?

The Spur

"Let's see what we've got here," Varas began.

> *Some say they're free because no one controls them.*
> *When I'm told of horses with no owners, I think of their*
>   *riders.*
> *Whoever nails your shoe and cinches your saddle*
> *Has a rider on his back with a sharp-spurred boot.*

"You want to explain that to me?"

"Explain what?" Benito looked up from the book he was reading

"Why this isn't published. And why the paper is torn and damp and has a soda bottle stain."

Benito shrugged and went on reading. After a minute he answered.

"Because we ran out of beer, the only thing in your *pinche* fridge is a quart bottle of flat Coca-Cola, there aren't any napkins, and I didn't want to stain the wood of your favorite table."

"Not my favorite, *güey*, my only one."

Varas crossed the room and sat down on the floor facing his friend, who was sprawled face down on the couch.

"Can I ask what it is you're writing?"

"A book of aphorisms."

"And that'll put food on the table?"

"I'm pitching some editors the idea that aphorisms are about to be the flavor of the month. Flash fiction is done, aphorisms are next. They're the germ that produces everything else: story, plot, dialogue, characters. Condensed information for people in a hurry. And, another hook, no royalties to pay. Tell me how these sound to you:

> *"Not even a cannonball in your face could wake you up, / if you're the calculated result of instantaneous repetition.*
> *"I regret trading cinnamon for a shell with no smell."*
> *"Still starry-eyed at thirty? An idiot disguised as a mule."*

Varas stretched out and stared at the ceiling, where he saw enormous green stains. He thought he ought to do something about this because there had to be a leaky pipe and any day now the ceiling would collapse. But what he did instead was to go on talking with his friend, though without taking his eyes away from the shapes he was finding amid the green.

"And how is that going?" he asked while discovering a belly dancer standing on one leg, which made his question sound a bit lackadaisical since he was concentrating on figuring out what kept her from falling.

"Badly. So far I haven't convinced anyone. Maybe in Barcelona, but here nobody will take the bait." Del Pliego sat up in the couch and looked at his friend. "Speaking of which, what are you doing here at home? Shouldn't you be at work?"

"I got fired. If you can't sell anyone on the book of aphorisms or publish those poems, we'll be on the flat Coke diet for a while."

"What happened?" del Pliego asked, following Varas's eye toward the stains on the ceiling where he spotted a palm tree that made him think of Veracruz.

"Nobody cared that I found a woman dragging herself through a tunnel of slime, or that there are any such tunnels, because all they want to know about is Vinueza. It's less than three weeks to election day."

"But didn't you tell them Vinueza was carried off by those blind guys? Didn't you tell them about that article by Binns?"

"I told them all that, plus what I think, which is that the missing women have a lot to do with those guys, and that houses are collapsing all over Poso Wells because of the tunnels, which are almost everywhere by now. There's a city under the city. But you know what my editor said? That he was sick and tired of me and I'd better get my ass over to police headquarters to investigate some refrigerators and TVs stolen out of the cops' own warehouses by the janitors."

"And you said?" With an effort Benito tore himself away from the magnificent waterfalls and jacaranda trees he'd found on the ceiling, so he could look his friend in the eye.

"That there was never anything worth finding out at police headquarters but if he wanted some street corner scribbler to quote official statements . . ."

"And that was the end of your job . . ."

"Poet, your powers of discernment never cease to amaze me."

Just then the apartment door opened and the woman came in with the dog. Varas had made a leash from a piece of rope, and since the third day after their arrival, the pair had been taking daily walks around the neighborhood, with Varas always hoping that something they saw would provoke some kind of reaction from her. Témoc watched out for her and took charge of leading her back to the house. Varas's finances were in a state of collapse because he'd spent all his savings on clothes and shoes for her.

"*Güey*, close your mouth before a fly gets in. Go get her a glass of water," Varas said, while he got up and led the woman to the couch. Benito handed her the glass, then took Varas by the arm and over to the window.

"You're going to find out who she is and where she came from, right?" Benito asked.

"If you decide to help me, it'll get done sooner rather than later," Varas answered in a whisper.

Benito gave him a long look.

"You want me to help you? To go out there with you?" he said, his voice cracking.

"Are you deaf, poet? That's what I said." Without another word he walked over to the stereo. He put on the Café Tacuba CD. He returned to the window, pulled out a pack of Belmonts with only one remaining, lit it, and heard, "You say I'm crazy because I laugh when maybe I ought to cry/you say I'm crazy because I've cried when happiness was like a lullaby," but the words were obscured by the downstairs neighbor's raspy cough starting up just as it did every day at this time—the cough, then the loud clearing of his throat, then the sound of him spitting phlegm out the window. Neighborhood noises, nothing new, yet they always took him by surprise and sent his thoughts in strange directions. Today those had to do with Benito. Varas was thinking that if anything could push his friend into picking up the thread of his life where he'd dropped it, this would be the ticket, because clearly the woman interested him. He was also thinking that he knew more about Benito and his family than about himself or his own. While the cigarette burned away, he went over Benito's story again. He'd been born in Veracruz, not Mexico City, but his true fate would have had him born in Guayaquil, if not for the maneuvers of a bureaucrat with a grudge who'd decided to twist his life story out of shape. Benito's grandfather, as his friend had told him the story, was a supporter of the Spanish Republic who had escaped from the Old World with nothing but a book of Antonio Machado's poetry under his arm. The book was worn out from reading, and it opened to the most-fingered pages:

> Sing with me, sing it, the nothing that we know,
> From the obscure sea we come, to the unknown sea we
> go . . .
> Between, the haunting enigma, three chests with keyless
> locks
> Tell me, what does the word say? And the water among the
> rocks?

With Machado under his arm and a few pesos in his pockets, Benito's future grandfather sought refuge in Guayaquil in the home of the Demetrio Aguilera Malta, whom he had met in Madrid in '36. He soon felt he couldn't have chosen a better place. He liked Guayaquil immediately, its topography, the gaze of its women, the pervasive smell of ripening fruit. His friend took him to meetings where the dust in the air still held the aroma of coffee and the lilt of voices carried him away from the war and the horrors that he had lived. He was sure that the more time he spent in this city, the faster he would lose the doleful look that he still couldn't recognize as his own. When his memories started to blur, he knew he wanted to stay. He began trying to legalize his status but, on the advice of friends, rather than following the standard red tape he went straight to the head of the immigration department of the Foreign Ministry, a writer himself, with a letter of reference from Aguilera Malta. The man, with almond eyes and the air of a fallen French aristocrat, welcomed him with excessive warmth and told him that for a friend of an author of such stature, he would do whatever was in his power. What was in his power was to avenge himself for the fact of Aguilera Malta being the better writer, which had long ago cost him a girlfriend who preferred Aguilera's skillful prose despite his ungainly appearance, over the bureaucrat's starchy, antique style, disregarding his noble bearing and chiseled face. In red ink, the bureaucrat stamped "communist" on every page of Señor Pliego's application for legal residence, as a result of which both visa and residence were denied. Thus began a pilgrimage that led Benito's grandfather to Mexico, where he started a newspaper, *La Verdad*, on the Gulf coast, which was why, in due course, Ecuadorian literature, and especially that of Demetrio Aguilera, won followers in that corner of the world. The bureaucrat's spleen could never pardon the Spaniard's good fortune or the diffusion of the Ecuadorian writer's work. He continued to pound his stamp with ever more vitriol onto any documents that passed before him, while in Veracruz they read his rival's stories to the strains of danzón floating on the gentle sea breeze—and old Pliego, smoking Cuban cigars and sipping mezcal, never tired of saying that the worst-intentioned plans oft went astray. He married a local woman, and in their family home flowered the nostalgic memory of a mythical and brotherly Ecuador. When their son fell in love, it was with a woman from that country, from the province of Manabí, whose ship had anchored in Veracruz en route to New Orleans. The fruit of this love was Benito, who spent his infancy in Portoviejo and his youth in the D.F., where, after reading many poems, he became a poet himself. Since then he had devoted himself to writing while taking whatever jobs came his way. One of those took him to Veracruz, where he stowed away on the *MV Rabolú*, a Panamanian-flag freighter on its way to Valparaíso, which made a stop to take on cargo in Guayaquil, where he barely escaped being discovered. Though he was tempted to disembark where he ought to have been born, a sixth sense warned him this was a last resort, to be used only in case of necessity. He continued on to Chile and spent some years working on the banana boats that smuggled Chilean wine to Ecuador and Mexico. On one such voyage, while the ship was still taking on its bootleg cargo in Valparaíso, he picked the wrong moment to check the setting of the thermostat in the engine room. He stumbled into a settling of scores between two crewmen and ended up with a knife in his shoulder blade. The lowlife of a captain, seeking to avoid trouble with authorities, ordered the ship to sail straight for Guayaquil without getting medical attention for Benito. In the Ecuadorian port he was abandoned on the dock, with a broken jaw and the knife still in his body, among some crates of apples and grapes on the assumption that he was dead. The port police sent him to the morgue, which was where Varas saw him for the first time. He was on the crime beat at the time, so every morning he went to the morgue to find out what had happened the night before. This being an especially slow morning, Varas passed the time waving off the horseflies that had come with Benito from the docks and kept settling on his face. His was the only corpse resting on the six cement tables of the autopsy room.

"So, this guy?" Varas asked.

"We don't know, they brought him in half an hour ago. No papers. We're waiting for the police to sign off on him before we open him up," answered a man eating a cheese sandwich, with breadcrumbs on his lips.

"So, I take it you never get indigestion?" Varas asked while looking at the other doctor, farther off, who was spreading blackberry jam on a buttered slice of bread.

"Varitas, you can see the answer for yourself," that one said, sucking on his fingertip.

Varas shrugged and asked the one nearby, "Where'd they find him?" while pulling out his notebook to write it up.

"On the docks, he was tossed between crates of Chilean apples."

"That should make the fucker tasty. Want a bite of him, Varas?" the doctor who was still sucking jam off his fingertip said.

Varas started toward that doctor with doubled fists, but the other one got between them to head him off.

"Ignore the guy, Varas. He's never had a girlfriend and he's spent all his time since med school with corpses. You should pity him, not get mad."

Varas looked at his watch and decided he didn't have time for fighting with a pair of degenerates, so he made his rounds of the hospitals instead. Around noon he got to the Luis Vernaza, next to the former prison by the shore, and there he found the corpse he'd seen in the morgue, waiting in a hallway in the emergency ward. He went looking for a nurse.

"This one?" asked. "He wasn't dead after all?"

The woman looked through her charts and finally answered, "Broken jaw and a knife wound in the shoulder that's made him lose a lot of blood."

"Sorry, miss, I didn't ask for his diagnosis, I mean why isn't anybody taking care of him?"

"Because nobody has come to say they'll pay his bill," she answered before hurrying down the hall.

Varas was about to make a scene when he took full note of his surroundings: burned-out lightbulbs, long lines, gaunt figures slumped in beat-up old chairs, and in all the hallways, three patients per cot. Instead of writing stupid pieces on wounds and murder victims, he should be sticking pins in the eyelids of those who had the power to change this daily sight. Or taking direct action, putting bombs under their SUVs. He ran after the woman.

"I'll be responsible, miss," he said.

"Go to the desk and give them your ID, then they'll give you a number." Still walking, the woman pointed out an area where more than eighty people were waiting to be called.

"Why not just put all the corpses out to tan in the sun?" Varas yelled down the crowded hallway of Luis Vernaza, but everyone just looked away. He went over to the man who had been left for dead that morning and took his pulse, finding hardly any. He pulled out his cellphone and decided it was time to collect some favors, so he dialed the number of a college friend who was now the son-in-law of the Minister of Health. He kept track of the time on the wall clock in the hall. In less than five minutes the wounded man was in the operating room. While the surgeons were busy, Varas went to revisit the dynamic duo at the morgue. They were in the middle of an autopsy, and he was sorry he hadn't waited outside. The smell was worse than a garbage dump in summer at high noon.

"Easy, Varas, this guy had hepatitis, see the color of his liver, here?" Just then the other doctor lifted out his intestines. "And he hadn't finished digesting his last meal."

"Never mind, you Neanderthals. I just want to know what happened with this morning's corpse." Varas covered his nose and mouth with one hand.

"Simple, Varitas, somebody didn't do their job right, and we almost took the electric saw to one that was still alive and kicking. But since we're professionals, we noticed the corpse was moving its eyelids so it couldn't be all that dead. We found a pulse, and before the cops arrived we'd already sent him to Luis Vernaza. Nobody cared, everything's fine, and then suddenly we got twenty very dead ones, thanks to the express buses of the Cruz del Sur line."

Varas was halfway out the door when they called him back.

"Listen, Varas, next time you write an article, write about the sonofabitch soulless bus drivers. Here's a piece of information for you. When we get one of them on the table, the first thing we do is look for it, but nothing, not even an ounce. They really are soulless, on the word of a well-educated scientist, and your paper can quote me in headlines as big as you like. If it weren't for the bus drivers, I'd have time for the occasional cigar once in a while, but they're relentless. Can't get even half a cigarette in, you hear me?"

On his way out Varas decided that the pathologists were not as maladjusted as he'd thought. When he got to the hospital, he was given a bill itemizing everything used in the operation: anesthesia, gauze, gloves, all in detail. They told him to go pay at the cashier's office; they also gave him another list with everything the patient would need during the rest of his hospital stay: analgesics, drips, anti-inflammatories, antibiotics; they told him to go buy those at a pharmacy, and they gave him a form to take over to the blood bank to make a donation, because the man who'd been stabbed had required several pints. When he returned, somewhat dizzy and with a bandage on his arm, Benito was out of surgical recovery, in a ward with eight other patients. He was very weak and his jaw was wired shut. Three days later they discharged him because they needed the bed, and all Varas could do was take him home. The circumstances were strange, but so was life. For three weeks Varas fed him through a straw, this man he didn't know from Adam who couldn't tell him anything. But one day, somewhat recovered, he mimed a request for pencil and paper, with which he wrote: "If you have eyes to see, turn them inward. Your only room is the room you've got; a darkened shack can be your castle, the axis around which you spin. But if you spend all your time inside yourself, you'll end up thinking that's all there is."

"Hey," Varas said enthusiastically, "you're a poet! What's your name?"

"Benito," he wrote.

Varas shook his hand. "*Encantado.* Glad to meet you. But you're turning white as a ghost so let's leave it for now," Varas added, fearful of the pallor creeping over the man.

From then on, the words on paper kept flowing, day by day.

> *Perseverance is virtue and damnation. 'The pursuit of ruin*
> *is the path to salvation,' a poet said.*
> *Hunger and cold may be our lot, but dissatisfaction is a*
> *knife we plunge into ourselves.*
> *A small, poor world, desire's honeycomb. It incites us, it*
> *satisfies us, and it buries us, too.*

When Benito was well enough to talk, he told Varas the whole story of what had happened to him. Since he was still weak, Varas got him work that he could do without leaving the apartment. The poet found himself writing for various cultural supplements, proofreading theater and concert programs, editing algebra texts for a private school, writing on movies and TV for a national paper. But when he had recovered enough and Varas proposed they go talk to the publisher of the paper where he worked, Benito said no. He didn't explain, and Varas didn't press him. Once in a while he'd go out to the store, and he'd go as far as the corner to buy the paper, and when he found a room for rent nearby, he moved so as not to trouble Varas further, although he held onto the apartment keys. He never ventured farther than four blocks away. Varas kept on finding jobs for him but aside from that, he decided Benito would have to deal with his own problem, whatever it was. Varas believed the answers to everything were usually in plain sight—sometimes obvious, sometimes not—but this didn't make the path to follow any easier. Besides, he wasn't a poet and couldn't explain things. You had to deal with your own fears, or you'd wind up resenting the world. And then someone else would have to take the blame.

✧ ✧ ✧

"Where do we start?" Benito asked.

Varas, who was a man from a bygone era, had two Polaroids of the woman. He gave one to his friend and kept the other. They were standing in the vacant lot.

"You go downhill, I'll go up. We'll meet here in three hours." He hesitated before continuing, but finally said what he wanted to say without beating around the bush.

"Or if you want, I'll go with you."

Benito didn't say anything, but he shook his head from left to right.

"Okay, back here at noon."

The poet set off down the street. The first two hours didn't yield anything. Everybody was on edge from all the soldiers still making the rounds of the neighborhood, clear ly unhappy and acting more like hired killers than legal authorities. Meanwhile, the tension with Salém's men had only increased. Three weeks after Vinueza's disappearance, there was no point in their coming into people's houses to search for him, but few denied them entrance for fear of repercussions. Bella, however, had opened a new battlefront after one of her sons found a piece of paper on the street bearing the same symbols painted on the houses that had been searched. The list was long but it showed that among the more than twenty messages coded in apparently innocent designs were instructions for burglarizing houses:

a circle surrounding a triangle meant only after 8:00 a.m.; two lines inside a circle meant only women live here; and there were eighteen more like that. Bella had invited her neighbors over to hear about her discovery but only three women came, one of them her friend Rosa. Then she'd taken the sheet of paper to the soldiers and asked them to compare the signs with those painted on the houses, to see for themselves that they matched up and thus have evidence against Salém. They ignored her and when she demanded to speak to the officer in charge of the operation, he made light of her complaint and argued that their mission was to find Vinueza, not to get involved in the barrio's quarrels. Before declaring their meeting over, he counseled resignation.

"Señora, I'm a great believer in the Lord's design, and you should be, too. Ask Him and you shall receive. And don't worry so much. Have you been robbed?"

Bella shook her head.

"Then stay out of it. Let everyone stick to his own business."

"Colonel, I think that whoever taught you your faith has done their job poorly, because from what I can see, you don't understand anything. But that's not my problem, your beliefs are up to you and you do what you want with them. I have my rights and you're here to look after the security of the citizens. I'm a citizen and I expect you to do your job."

"Do you have documents to prove that?"

"I was born in this country, Colonel. That's all I need."

"Listen, little lady, you seem a bit weak in the head. That's not my problem, you hear? My problem is finding Vinueza."

"Who pays you, that lawyer's companies or the Armed Forces of Ecuador?"

"Señora, don't provoke me. If you don't leave, I'll have to arrest you."

"Colonel, beliefs can drive a person crazy. I want your name, because this is not going to end here."

"Old busybody, are you trying to tell me you have contacts in the government?" The officer laughed, then straightened his shoulders. "Colonel Alcíbar Peña at your service."

He turned his back and went on his way, but not before scolding the corporal who had fetched him to speak with her. All that had happened a few days before the poet and Varas came with their photos of the unknown woman, and it was one more reason why the cooperation they got was almost zero. Very few people opened their doors, and those who did were highly suspicious. About 11 a.m. the poet knocked on Bella Altamirano's door. He showed her the photo and asked whether she could identify the person.

"And who are you?" the woman in the doorway asked him.

"A friend," Benito said.

"If you're such a good friend, why don't you know her name?"

He liked the way this woman talked back.

"So you know her?" the poet asked.

"What makes you think that?"

"Your question. If you didn't know anything, you wouldn't care who I am."

Bella smiled.

"That could be. So who are you?"

"Let me buy you a soda and I'll tell you."

Bella put her hand to her face to be sure no lock of hair was covering her scar. No, she had her hair in a bun.

"You know, I can't right now, but what I'll tell you is . . ."

"Maybe some other time," Benito interrupted.

Bella ignored him and went on. "This girl lived here, around the corner with her parents. Less than a year ago, she disappeared, just like that. Everybody had an opinion. You know what they say: small town, big hell. I think she was from Manabí, or anyway that's where her parents went after she didn't turn up. Do you know where she is? Did somebody find her?"

"And her name? Do you remember it?"

"Valentina. Valentina, that was her name."

✧ ✧ ✧

At the other end of the settlement, Varas had thrown in the towel. Either nobody knew anything, or everybody was hiding something, and he was in no mood to guess which. He walked to Montenegro's house and was lucky to find him at home. Varas told the old man everything that had happened since they'd last seen each other. As Montenegro was getting Varas's forgotten keys, the reporter fell asleep. When he woke up, startled, he asked the time and found that only five minutes had passed.

"What's wrong with you, Gonzalo?"

He liked Montenegro, the only person who had ever called him by his first name—only his mother and Montenegro, that is. With this good man, he felt safe enough to confess his fears. He'd spent too many days inside of them and getting nowhere.

"Don Jaime, I think I bit off more than I can chew. I've

got no idea what's behind all this. And I'm in it alone"—he lowered his head and was silent, then recovered—"well, one friend and I"—and then, smiling—"and a woman who doesn't say a word, and a dog."

"What about me? I'm not flesh and blood?"

"Okay," Varas blushed. "The five of us, then."

Montenegro handed him a glass of aguardiente. A tiny glass, like a thimble almost. "My daughter gave me these, they're from Turkey," he said before Varas could ask.

Varas realized he knew nothing about Montenegro. Confused, he was about to say something when the old man stopped him.

"Come with me, Gonzalo, I've got something to tell you."

In the backyard were sheets of brightly colored translucent paper piled on an old wooden table.

"The kids across the street, it's their birthday party tonight and I promised to make them sky lanterns. Do you know how?"

"No, I never learned. When I was a kid my grandfather made them, but I haven't seen one in years."

While Montenegro folded the papers with expert hands, he began to muse aloud, as if their previous conversation had floated away, and now they were in some timeless place.

"You know, Gonzalo, there's a question that's more for philosophers than for old men like me, but it keeps me awake at night. If you forget things, is it the same as if they never happened?"

When Montenegro finished making the balloon he plucked a piece of straw from the ground and lit it on fire, placing it under the diamond-shaped paper construction.

He and Varas watched the lantern fill with hot air and rise up into currents that lifted it toward the clouds. When it was nothing but a speck, Montenegro turned to face him.

"Last night, in the middle of the night when I couldn't sleep, I went outside. You know what I saw, in the street?"

The reporter didn't answer. In the distance, a series of firecrackers exploded one after another.

"If my eyes and nose didn't deceive me, Vinueza walked right by me. Surrounded by men with rattles on their legs and stinking to high heaven."

PART TWO

AMAZONAS AND NACIONES UNIDAS

Press Conference

The Salón Altavista in the basement of the Hotel Dann Carlton was packed with reporters. The few chairs set out in the small room had been commandeered by photographers and videographers aiming their cameras at a long table covered by a starched white tablecloth, behind which sat Vinueza and his five former kidnappers. The blind men's beards had been cut short, and their long white manes were brushed backward and held in place by immense quantities of hair gel. They were clad in tunics a celestial shade of blue. Vinueza, meanwhile, was stuffed into a sea-blue suit at least one size too small for him. With his red hair the shade of horsemeat, he looked like a sausage produced by some fly-by-night butcher shop. He wore a yellow tie dotted with purple and displayed a cool disinterest in the goings on around him, though his breathing was irregular and even gasping at times. He'd been rushed to the press conference directly from the airport and was having trouble with Quito's altitude, on top of everything else that had happened since his liberation. From the moment he'd left the subterranean prison to step into a midnight taxi taking him and his kidnappers to his gated residence in Samborondón, the most unusual things had happened. He'd toyed with the idea of having the blind men arrested, but first he'd gone straight to his study for a dose of illumination from his personal stash of heavenly powders. Then he'd realized the ancient men were his ticket to the Presidency. Once that idea took hold, he'd spent all his energy fleshing it out, right up to the time of the press conference the next afternoon. He'd called José María, the archdiocese of Guayaquil, his contacts in the electoral and constitutional courts, three Supreme Court justices, and all the TV channels. It had been three a.m. when he picked up the phone, but what did that matter to him?

✧ ✧ ✧

Varas was worried. He and Benito had met up as planned and exchanged their latest discoveries: that the woman's name was Valentina, and that Vinueza, no longer disappeared, was expected to appear on TV at any moment. The poet suggested buying a bottle to celebrate. Varas thought that what his friend wanted to commemorate was not what he'd discovered but his return from who-knew-what personal hell. Therefore he accepted the proposal. They pooled what money they had in their pockets to buy a bottle of Clan MacGregor, the only Scotch produced within the borders of Ecuador, better known for its marathon hangovers than for any exceptional flavor. Benito and Varas held their celebration in the Parque de las Iguanas. It was a very pleasant afternoon—mothers taking their children for walks, tourists snapping photos, old folks absorbed in daily confabulations—and the two of them drinking from the bottle disguised within a paper bag to avoid the attention of police. Despite the worry nagging at Varas, he'd never seen his friend so calm, so he went along with celebrating the occasion. At any rate, about the latest news, what more could he do than speculate? And after more than half the bottle was gone, his speculations had still not led to any conclusions.

"What do you think Vinueza will do?" he asked.

"What are you talking about, *mamón?* I've seen iguanas better looking and better behaved than that guy," said Benito, who would have preferred another topic of conversation.

Varas pointed to an old iguana perched in a tree, looking more serious and dignified than any member of the national legislature.

"See?" Benito told him. "You didn't have to look very far. The one who's really good-looking, though, is Bella."

"And who's that?" Varas asked after taking another swig.

"The one who told me about Valentina."

"I thought it was Valentina you were interested in," Varas said.

"And get in your way? No thanks, *güey.* I wish you could see the expression on your face when you look at her."

Varas didn't answer. An iguana scooted across his leg, raising goosebumps.

But that was five hours ago. Now he was seated in front of the TV with Témoc, Valentina, and a terrible sense of unease. Where was Benito now, he wondered. The last thing he remembered was that, on parting, he'd told his friend not to look down when he got to his feet, because that might make him dizzy, and he'd fall. What was that about? Fall? Where to? And who was he to be giving this advice? A tightrope walker? An acrobat?

✧ ✧ ✧

It took a while for the press conference to get going. The press and radio reporters crowded around the table that the organizers, showing poor judgment, had placed very close to the wall so that no one could get behind it. After a brief tussle, the TV reporters ended up winning, as usual. Their companies paid the government $365 a month for the use of their assigned frequencies throughout the country, and that bit of small change gave them complete control over the images and events that Ecuadorians got to see. It was no more or less logical than anything else in the country. They had power and didn't hesitate to use it, just as they were doing now to crowd out their colleagues, elbowing past any who dared to block the view of the cameras and thus of the public. That public included Varas, the woman, and the dog. When they first turned on the TV, static interrupted the opening minutes of the broadcast. Once they could see and hear, there was Vinueza, microphone in hand.

"The country is in a terrible state, but we're going to turn it around. 360 degrees."

A barely audible question came from an unseen reporter: "You mean, you're going to turn us in a complete circle and we'll end up in the same place?"

Vinueza ignored this. "We're at the edge of an abyss," he pronounced, "and we need to take a step forward."

"Off the cliff?" the same reporter asked.

There were sounds of a scuffle, a falling microphone,

and then Vinueza's voice again. His face had not left the screen.

"But before speaking, I want to say a few words . . ."

Feet could be heard shuffling, and someone coughed. Varas got up and went to the kitchen, came back with a mug of water, and began talking to the dog.

"Are you listening, Témoc? The number of stupidities per second? Don't you find it hard to believe?"

"I have my own opinions, very strong ones, but I'm not always in agreement with them," Vinueza said in answer to a question that the microphone did not catch. His gaze was lost somewhere in the infinite.

✧ ✧ ✧

A few blocks from the Carlton, on Avenida Naciones Unidas near the corner of Amazonas, stood the department store Almacenes Japón. This was one of the darkest corners in the northern part of the capital. Although the televisions in the store's display windows remained on, at that hour the beings who ventured out that way were few. They could be counted on the fingers of one hand and belonged, in general, to two groups. The first was composed of bewildered drunks who staggered out of the High Horse, the karaoke-disco-whorehouse hidden behind a nearby gas station. The second was made up of rats from the hordes that took possession of the area's parking lots once the cars departed. Tonight there was a man with a gash in his forehead, barely able to stand. He had spent more than half his wages on whiskey and on Sun Yi, a Panamanian-Chinese-Ecuadorian teenager who had come to the capital from Quevedo to earn herself some quick money and whose favorite reading matter was Dale Carnegie's *How to Win Friends and Influence People*, a copy of which she had personally fortified so it would not come apart in her hands during many nighttime readings after her hours of hard labor. She had come to the capital to enroll in a course at Quito's Og Mandino Institute, because her reading had taught her the importance of study as a means for getting ahead in life. Carnegie had persuaded her of the importance of specialization, too, and therefore she had chosen the path of "unusual methods." She always traveled with a snake in her possession, a fer-de-lance from which, every morning, she milked a quantity of venom into a small glass jar that had once held honey. She used the viper, in an innovative way, to petrify her clients. When this failed, she had recourse to her other specialty, "the lollipop," a term she'd learned from a friend who had traveled abroad. But the man now watching the press conference while clinging to a streetlamp to keep himself upright had not experienced any of the nymphet's delights. When he'd entered her room and found a cot, a lamp covered with a red silk handkerchief, a chair, and the box where she kept the viper, he had burst into tears. Putting Carnegie's teachings rapidly into practice, Sun Yi slid off his pants while the man mumbled something about the pointlessness of life and the girl thought how wrong he was, given what reliable sources said about the connection between time and money. When she started removing his shoes, more for aesthetic reasons than any other, the man took her by the arms and Sun Yi thought she was finally getting somewhere, but what he did was to seat her on his lap so he could put his head on her shoulder and fall asleep. The teenager began to get annoyed. When she took off her blouse and offered him a mouthful of *guaitambo* (which, she had been told by some girls from Ambato, was the local term for the peaches grown in the mountains, and, given her resolve to always have the right information at the right time, she had noted this on a pad where she wrote down all sorts of useful data for later memorization), the man called her *pobrecita*. Poor little thing. This unleashed a storm inside the room that continued down the hallway of the second floor of the High Horse.

"There's nothing 'poor' about anything to do with me!" she screamed while pounding his head with the point of her high-heeled shoe before pushing him down the stairs, not without first emptying his wallet in just compensation, she thought, for the time and services bestowed.

That was how he'd landed in front of the display window of the department store. But he couldn't hear anything or make any sense of the blind men on the screens of the twelve variously sized televisions before him—men who seemed to have stepped out of a bad 1970s version of *The Ten Commandments*— so he closed his eyes and fell asleep. Every so often he stirred enough to watch the silent press conference through half-closed eyes.

✧ ✧ ✧

From the start of the conference, the blind men had not opened their mouths. No one had asked who they were or what they were doing there, but given the tenor of the answers coming from Vinueza, the TV producers were going to have to choose between ending the news flash or resigning themselves to the audience clicking it off with their remotes.

"What do you believe in? Why do you want to be president?" a reporter called from the rear of the room.

"I think that if one knows what he believes in, that makes it much easier for him to answer questions. I can't answer your question." Vinueza said, after taking a drink from his water glass.

There was no attempt at a follow-up. In the uncomfortable silence, someone had the presence of mind to ask about the blind men.

"These men with you, who are they?"

Vinueza straightened in his chair and seemed to take on a new persona.

"They are wise men who have led me to understand that God wants me to be the next president of all Ecuadorians."

Just then some reporters who had barely taken part in the proceedings because they were trapped behind two Ionic columns characteristic of the hotel's over-the-top décor decided to emerge from their prison. In so doing, they bumped into the knees of one of the cameramen perched on a chair. The man lost his balance and his camera tilted, which allowed the audience to see, for a few seconds, the blind men's sandals and their strange ankle bracelets, composed of big seeds or the paws of desiccated animals. The director in the control room cut to a large sign advertising the hotel.

✧ ✧ ✧

In his semi-conscious state, the drunk recognized the sign and, since the post he was holding onto did not make for the best of mattresses, decided to walk in that direction.

✧ ✧ ✧

"I am aware of my weaknesses, but I trust in the power of God. I renew my vow to follow the path that He offers me, as a source of light for all Creation. He who lives in Christ is born again. For him, the ancient times have not passed, and a new world has arrived." So Vinueza described his recent encounter with Jesus.

"How did you escape electrocution?" asked a reporter only a few inches from the candidate.

"The fires of hell and the sulfur that rose from the wooden stage and fell from heaven only purified my commitment to our countrymen who are most in need. I am selected by the grace of God because I truly believe that He speaks through me."

"Why do you think you were chosen? It is known that there was a spike in voltage and, according to well-informed sources, a liquid conducted the current . . ."

"I will do all that is in my power to heal the human suffering that is so abundant and daunting," Vinueza interrupted.

At that moment, the five men who had remained silent began to murmur, producing a sound like that of hundreds of crickets at dusk. The reporters fell silent and the blind men began to speak, one at a time but threading and echoing their words, reproducing in the small room the sense of infinity from the tunnels of Poso Wells.

"Verily, verily, we say that ye shall see the sky split open."

"And the angels of God will rise and descend with the Son of Man."

"The ladder of divine Providence comes to Earth through the ministry of the angels."

"The ladder is the sign of the Christ's Reincarnation among the descendants of Jacob, who joined together humanity and the divine."

"As Christ is the true God and the true man."

✧ ✧ ✧

From the moment the men began to speak, Varas saw, Valentina had become agitated. She kept on shifting in her seat, her pupils shrunken and her eyes locked on the screen. She lifted Témoc onto her lap and ran her hand up and down his back, over and over. Only when her squirming brought her to the very edge of the couch did she finally stand up.

✧ ✧ ✧

"Are you suggesting that after the candidate came down the ladder from the helicopter, and after Señor Andrés Vinueza was saved, he became the incarnation of God?" a puzzled reporter asked.

At that moment the five men began to stamp their feet, causing such a racket that neither the reporters at the press conference nor the TV audience in their homes could hear above the jangling of their anklet-castanets. At this moment, Valentina began to scream and would not stop. Varas tried to comfort her but she brushed his arm from her shoulders. The downstairs neighbor began to pound his ceiling with a broomstick, and Témoc added to the confusion by starting up a howl. The woman moved closer to the television and finally touched her hand to the screen.

"It's them," she said in what was barely a whisper. "It's them."

✧ ✧ ✧

The drunk had reached Avenida República de El Salvador and was preparing to turn the corner toward the hotel when five police cruisers roared by, sirens blaring, almost grazing his leg as they took the corner at high speed. Once he regained his balance, he followed the sound for four blocks until he got to where they were parked. A sizeable crowd was gathered in the door of the hotel, holding candles and carrying signs that proclaimed Vinueza's divinity. The blind men emerged from the building in single file, walking toward a car with tinted windows waiting by the entrance. Vinueza had remained behind, arguing with someone with a face like an eel. Both men were yelling, but it was impossible to hear what they said. The drunk walked toward one of the bearded men and knelt down to touch his anklet rattles, which had been calling out to him like a bottle to a baby. When the blind man became of aware of his presence, he began kicking him, and the four others joined in. Vinueza came running out of the hotel and, with what agility his chubby body allowed, herded the blind men toward the car. The drunk lay on the curb, completely bloodied and unable to understand what had happened. In his right fist he clasped one of the rattles.

Minefields Express

"Andrés, don't throw this all away. Tell the driver to turn around. Come back so we can talk in peace and quiet," José María said by cellphone.

"I'll come back if the wise men can stay with me," Vinueza answered.

"What wise men? What are you talking about, Andrés? Didn't these wise men imprison you and beat you in some catacomb for three solid weeks?" José María responded impatiently.

"Only through suffering do we find truth."

"Okay, okay," José María said, trying to compose himself. "I'll rent them a room, but come back right away."

Once they were both at the check-in desk, José María took Andrés by the arm and led him toward the elevators.

"What about the blind men?" Vinueza protested.

"Someone will bring them up to a room right next to yours. Stop worrying about your blind men, and think about what to say to the Canadians. I don't know whether your sudden candidacy is going to appeal to them."

"Why not? It guarantees them a safe investment. Of

course, now I can't appear as a director of anything. How would you like to be General Manager of the Eagle Copper Corporation?"

Walking toward Room 802 alongside Vinueza, José María couldn't hide his joy at this news.

❖ ❖ ❖

"You know what bothers me? Just when you finally start to understand things, they go and change the rules on you," Benito said.

"Not always, *ñañito*. Sometimes it takes so long to understand that, by the time you get it, the opportunity has already passed you by.

"Hmm, so we've always got something to blame ourselves for? You want water?"

"Don't kid yourself, sweetie, I've got a friend who says that the trick is to be suicidal without killing yourself. Guilt isn't always personal. Just ice, *s'il vous plaît*."

❖ ❖ ❖

There were seven men gathered in the room. Men accustomed to buying, marketing, trading, and selling. Right now, international markets decreed that the commodity of the moment was copper. It was scarce, indispensable, and offered enormous profits. Making a deal with a corrupt government was just the icing on the cake of an excellent investment—albeit a volatile one. Therefore, only those who could demonstrate perseverance, patience, and discipline could get the necessary backing. The necessary concessions.

"We're delighted to find you in good health," said the man in an impeccable sea-blue suit accessorized with red silk handkerchief and tie. He was six and a half feet tall and his voice projected authority. Vinueza accepted the expression of goodwill, nodding like an obedient employee, and went on listening. José María stepped away to answer his phone.

"We're also very pleased to know that now we can formalize our agreement after the unfortunate delay." He had no accent, but something about the way he shaped his lips around the words suggested Spanish was not his first language. "After your inopportune disappearance, that is. We've had to wait three weeks to move ahead on acquiring the land, but I'm sure that with your presence, everything will be resolved."

"That's what I'm here for, Señor Holmes, you've got nothing to worry about. I'm going to have the documents drawn up right away. You can consider the land purchases in Intag as good as done. I just want to double check the figure. Are we still talking about 300,000 acres?"

"To begin with, yes." Holmes had cut the tip of his Romeo y Julieta, and the man alongside him held a lighter at the ready.

"You'll understand that my name can't appear in the company's founding documents, although we'll be shareholders through the holding company, of course."

"José María and my legal advisor can work that out. I know you're a man of your word."

Vinueza had grown fond of old-fashioned expressions in recent days, and to think of himself as that kind of man was particularly satisfying. He reached out his hand.

"You have my word on it, you certainly do."

115

✧ ✧ ✧

A bellhop led the five blind men to their accommodations, where, after asking whether everything was to their taste and receiving neither reply nor tip, he closed the door and left them alone. They found themselves in one of the hotel's four suites. In less than five minutes they managed to break all the lamps and decorations in the first room before moving on to the bath. There they admired the cool feel of the tile floor, and one of them found the spigot of the sink. They were startled by the warmth of the water that flowed out. When they found the bathtub control they opened it too, but once the initial surprise was past, they grew tired of standing up and putting their hands under the water, so they returned to the living room where some sat down in the scattered leather armchairs while others sprawled on the carpet, which they compared to the fleece of the llamas their ancestors had raised. They considered themselves well on their way toward their objective. Given their exhausting day, they soon feel asleep. What woke them was a knocking on the door—tentative at first, then more insistent.

"What is happening?" three of them said, moving their heads from side to side while the other two remained asleep.

The knocking stopped and footsteps filled the room.

"Don't you know you're flooding the place?" José María shouted at them, stepping over the men lying on the floor on his way to the bath, followed by several hotel staff with buckets and mops. When he came back, the cuffs of his pants were soaked, his face was red as a pepper, and his hands had formed into fists that wanted nothing more than to pound on his boss's new pets. Only the need to keep Vinueza on his side for the time being made it possible for him to maintain his self-control. The hotel manager was standing in the door.

"Charge any damages to our account," José María grumbled.

"We already have. But wouldn't you like me to find the gentlemen another room? Here we'll have to take up the carpet before the water sinks into the floor and destroys the ceiling of the room below."

"Couldn't you do that tomorrow? These gentlemen are extremely tired and weak, so moving them to another room now would be too much for their fragile state," said José María, thinking that over his dead body were they going to charge him for another suite, on top of the damages to this one and its daily rate.

The manager hesitated but then agreed. José María stayed where he was until the staff had finished cleaning up. The blind men, meanwhile, had retired to the bedroom farthest from the bath and closed the door. When the cleaning was done, José María left without a word and took the elevator in order to join Vinueza and the Canadians. The formalities completed, they were gathered around the room's mini-bar drinking Chivas Regal, and barely took notice of his arrival.

"My dear Andrés, I hope I may call you that?"

"Of course, Mr. Holmes."

"Are you acquainted with Lao Tse?"

"I haven't had the pleasure."

"A font of wisdom. Do you know what he says about governing?"

"No, actually, I don't."

"In Book Sixty, he says that ruling a great kingdom is like frying fish."

Since no answer was required, Vinueza took a long swallow of whiskey and nodded his agreement. José María thought this would be an opportune moment to interrupt.

"Andrés, could I speak with you for a minute?"

"Excuse me, Señor Holmes, I'll be right with you."

The two moved toward the door. José María recounted what had happened with the blind men.

"Go back and don't move till I get there, I'm almost finished here," Andrés ordered José María.

José María left and Vinueza headed back toward Holmes, who was speaking with a voice of authority that suggested some message was being delivered.

"True, true, in Plato's *First Alcibiades*, Socrates stresses the need to know oneself in order to govern ... Andrés, come on over, we're discussing the challenges you'll be confronting in the coming weeks."

Holmes took Andrés by the arm and drew him into the group.

❖ ❖ ❖

Sun Yi was not one given to taking unnecessary risks, but ever since expelling her most recent client at heel-point, she'd felt trapped in the High Horse. She decided she needed fresh air to clear her head. She put on a jacket to head out for a walk, though she wasn't sure of her location because she'd come directly from the airport in a taxi, and this was her first visit to the capital. Therefore, on the off chance of some unexpected difficulty, she put the box containing the fer-de-lance into her purse. That morning, due to an oversight, she had failed to milk the day's venom. She decided it would be best to walk on the median strip that separated the two lanes of traffic on Naciones Unidas, practically devoid of traffic at this hour. The chilly night air felt good, so she decided to walk to the Atahualpa Stadium, which she recognized in the distance, rising like a sizeable gourd from the Parque Carolina. She had crossed the Avenida de los Shyris when a black SUV with tinted windows stopped a few yards from her. Feeling uneasy, she tightened her hold on her purse and decided she could do without seeing the stadium close up tonight. She turned around and began retracing her steps. The car followed suit.

"Son of bitch," she whispered to herself, and decided she needed to change tactics if she were going to avoid becoming one more statistic of social disorder. Survival, she had learned, was all about adapting to circumstances. She walked to the edge of the median and waited for the car to come to her.

"And how might I be of service to the gentleman tonight?" she asked, leaning against the driver's door with her elbow on the partly opened window.

She could barely make out the eyes of the man driving. Someone in the back seat said something, and the door opened.

"Wait a minute, I always make the deal first, before getting into any stranger's car. About the monetary issues . . ."

At this point, Sun Yi remembered she was wearing slippers, sweatpants, a sweatshirt, and an old jacket, and had gathered her hair into a ponytail. Whoever had given the order to open the door wasn't thinking about negotiating any deal. She changed tactics again and got in. She found a chubby man with tiny hands who told her she just needed to cooperate and nothing would happen to her and in the morning they'd let her go. She didn't like the sound of that but decided to see where they were taking her before finding a way out. She didn't have much time to think, because in less than five minutes they stopped in front of a hotel with golden doors, and the little man told her to follow him. Which she did, still remaining silent. She didn't see anyone around to come to her aid, especially if the man was a guest here. Anyway, what could she say? That she'd been picked up on the street in the middle of the night and been brought to a luxury hotel? She followed him into the elevator.

"What do you want me to do? Tell me straight out, I'm sure we can come to a mutually satisfying agreement."

Silence was his only answer. The door opened and they walked down a hallway. They came to a room that, once inside, she could see was a disaster. Things strewn around the floor, carpets rolled up in the corners, and everything smelling like a trap. The little man told her to stay there, and disappeared down an inner hall. She used the opportunity to check the door, but it was locked. Soon the man returned and told her to follow him. They came to another room where a group of blind old men, half-dressed, were waiting. By now she had discarded every plan of action she'd turned over in her head, and she was starting to get quite nervous.

"What do they want?"

"Not much. Really, we could say it's very little. An heir." That's what the little man said as he edged back toward the door.

"What? You're going to leave me here? How long?" a worried Sun Yi asked as the men began to surround her.

"There's been a change of plans. You can leave in nine months." He stepped out and closed the door behind him.

"What??" Sun Yi's cries echoed off the walls of the half-destroyed room.

XI
The Bottom of the Empty Glass

"Are you planning on moving in?"

"Are you throwing me out?"

"Not at all, sweetie. Let's just say I'm asking because I don't know your situation but I have to work and this bed is my office, so if you don't get off of it I'll have to go on welfare, and you know how things are in this country— those kinds of amenities just don't exist."

"But it would be so easy to just stay in your bed, you know?"

"Especially since we didn't do everything we might have . . ."

"Ummm, are you going to throw that in my face again?"

"Admit it or not, the night was a little on the bizarre side. I'm not in the habit of rescuing guys who are drunk as a skunk before the cops pick them up, bringing them home, having them pass out and then get up in the middle of the night to start philosophizing and reciting poems."

"But you know something about reciting yourself, let me try to remember it:

But what happens at the precise moment

121

of giving birth?
What do we do
when it's more Monday than Friday
when our veins are more than a gallows?"

"I told you, I spent my teenage years reading poems. What else could I do, knowing I had to become someone else? And my best friend is a poet. His name is Villalba. Everything I recite is his."

"Where can I find his stuff?"

"I've got some loose pages and a bunch of napkins in an envelope, and my memory never fails me either. But books? Benito, darling, I think you're still plastered. What country are you living in?"

"Okay, I'm leaving, but only if you memorize this and recite it to your friend the next time you see him." The poet stood upright on the bed, very carefully seeking out the exact center and holding himself as stiffly as an orator. "Tell him it's in his honor."

No better disguise for the fierce than the pelt of the meek.
He who rules through terror is his subjects' slave. Only he
who kills with love can command your life.
The poet's saliva washes away the warrior's blood,
but no one cleans the one who does not resist,
whose blood flows into the conscience and stifles the breath.

To be a lion is no easy thing, but it's so much harder
to be a lion if you're a lamb.

The one watching from the chair by the night table stood and applauded and then walked toward the bed. The upper part of his face was made up with elaborate eye shadow, but below the nose everything was a pure act of will.

"In return, here's one from Villalba to you. When I'm done, then, *ciao ciao* brown cow."

The man who called himself Martirio smiled his most dazzling smile and moved his hands like castanets to perfectly accompany his words of farewell. Then he stretched out an arm so Benito could help him up onto the bed, and he waited for the poet to take a seat in the chair before beginning his recitation.

Everything is like a cry linked
to the type of music
in your veins
music of birds
of a feather
winged fairies with cocks in hand
like me,
slipping into another morning
once more bent and broken
5:30 in my ear
the cylinder spinning
bullets in the chamber:
these fatal memories
of butterflies and ugly christs,
when did all this happen?
but I unwind
and go on unwinding
far from the rendezvous.
What happened? How many
boys and girls sacrificed their retinas
for just a momentary glimpse of you,

just the sight of you,
it's your hand,
an infinite sacrilege
but it sounds the alarm
and this sonofabitch dawn is worse than a dagger,
the booze still running
like a ring of fire
down my throat
and in spite of the warning
when there was still
time to waste

✧ ✧ ✧

"Listen, guys, we've got to get organized. This way is never going to work."

Sun Yi had judged that she could turn the tide in her favor if she took charge of what was going to ensue. After all, no one had stayed to oversee things, and here she was in a room with a group of decrepit old men who were blind to top it off. For once, she had figured wrong, but luckily for her, not completely. The blind men were fossils but they were determined and they had her outnumbered five to one. All that she had in her favor was that none of them could get an erection. They tried but they couldn't, and since she had no idea what was going on, she devoted what time she had to thinking about how she could get out of there. It wouldn't be that hard, she just had to create some kind of distraction and then call the front desk and say, as calmly as she could manage, that her door wasn't working and she needed someone to open it. Someone would come and she'd walk out, as simple as that. She didn't take immediate action because the blind men seemed fairly confused and disoriented, but then her luck ran out. They grabbed her by the arms and legs and laid her down on the floor and began tearing her clothes to shreds. She hadn't let go of her purse all night, and now with the men's naked, ruined bodies all over her, she decided things had gone too far and she pulled the box holding the fer-de-lance from her purse. She rolled on the carpet and unhooked the top of the box to let the viper drop onto the sunken belly of one of the blind men. The viper did not slither very far, because, feeling herself threatened, she sank her teeth into the first protuberance she found, which was the limp member of one of the men. The scream that came out of his toothless mouth scorched the nerves of his comrades who crawled toward him to try to help. The scream must have penetrated into the corridor because almost immediately the door opened and Vinueza came in. Sun Yi dashed out, half dressed. She took one look back inside before disappearing for good, and what she saw was a bruised and trembling patriarch dying in the arms of the little man. She decided, while vanishing down the nearby streets in the first light of day, that city life was not for her. She would take the first bus that left the station in the direction of Salango, not even going back to Quevedo. She'd rather help her family with the fishing than get involved in the kind of dark doings that had unfolded, one after another, since she'd come to the capital. Her faith in Dale Carnegie had grown weaker and weaker since she'd found herself in need of putting it to the test.

And even if Carnegie was right, so what? She had to stay alive.

PART THREE

THE
CLOUD
FOREST

Checkmate

"We've got the first concession. It's for 20,000 acres, Eagle I and Eagle II."

"And the price?"

"$110,000, no expiration date. We were the only bidders in the auction."

"Congratulations, Vinueza."

"The only problem is that too many people had gotten wind of it, so I was almost lynched when I showed up. There's a public letter opposing the concession, signed by the local authorities, the mayor, the Cotacachi County council, and every grassroots organization in the county."

"Which will no longer be a problem once you're elected at the polls on Sunday," Holmes replied.

Vinueza was not as convinced, but he wasn't going to talk the gringo out of that belief. He'd reported what happened, which was as far as his responsibility went. What the letter said to him, on quick reading, was that open pit mining would turn the forest into a desert. Removing all the soil to unearth the copper would mean shoveling out sixty tons a day. Goodbye trees, orchids, birds. Goodbye cloud forest, in short. Well, *bon voyage*, because looking at the bright side, he would make millions and so would the Canadians. The next few days would tell the tale. Something was going to happen before the week was out, he was sure of that. The atmosphere was too heated, the residents of the Intag region had been given the run-around for too long. The area granted to Eagle Copper Corporation lay within the Cotacachi-Cayapas Ecological Reserve, which the notary who drew up the documents had overlooked but the local people and officials did not. The outcome remained to be seen. Well, there was a time and place for everything.

✧ ✧ ✧

Varas had a decision to make about what to do. Once Valentina had calmed down and he'd turned off the TV, she started to talk and didn't stop till nearly dawn. Varas was dumbfounded. He had trouble accepting all of it, yet he had no doubt it was true. It was unheard-of, monstrous, and staggering—but believable, absurdly so. Though Valentina couldn't make even a rough estimate of how many women were down in the tunnels, she knew there were a lot, of all ages, the majority of them driven to madness to one degree or another. She didn't know how long they'd been prisoners, how long they'd gone without seeing the light of day. During her time down there she'd spoken with very few of them. They avoided each other because in the darkness you couldn't tell who was who until someone was practically on top of you. The blind men didn't always wear their rattles, and their assaults in those dark passageways were frequent and common. As soon as she'd been kidnapped and dragged underground, her captors had taken off her clothes. The whole time she was there she'd had no way to cover herself. The encounters with the men were grotesque: while they assaulted her, they recited their convoluted speeches about the perpetuation of their civilization and its customs. They repeated the history of trading their cool, fresh Andean valley for the suffocating heat and damp chill of the tunnels—knowing that their mission was to prevent their people's disappearance on the day soon to come when the flames of Cotopaxi would flow like rivers of fire down the volcano's flanks as the elders had foreseen. They had moved to the estuary to survive, and this they had done, though without success in their desperate race against extinction. This they repeated, endlessly, as if trying to keep their story alive. Just as in the past they had been overcome by the sudden onset of blindness, now for more than half a century their seed had failed to produce life. Valentina had never heard any babies crying in the tunnels where she was imprisoned, and she, in spite of the many assaults, had never become pregnant.

Those five wretched men were the perpetrators of the crime of holding hundreds of women captive. Now they were advising the future president, in what manner nobody knew, but it clearly offered them the possibility of escape.

✧ ✧ ✧

Holmes had never doubted that Vinueza would manage to get the concession granted, but he did have his doubts that this was the man to control the population opposed to mining in the area. Therefore, without the candidate's knowledge, he had contracted a retired general as the Eagle Cooper Corporation's community relations officer. Gen.

Jorge Villavicencio, with a past that no one could call un-blemished, had carte blanche to do whatever he thought necessary to dissuade the opponents of mining develop-ment. Getting right to work, he assembled a group of un-employed men in the area of Vinces, promising them land in the cloud forest if they'd undergo a course of basic train-ing in an army camp to prepare them to get rid of some pesky squatters, after which they could take legal possession of their new property. What the retired general did not tell the nearly sixty men he hired, outfitted in camouflage and armed with machetes, chainsaws, pistols, knives and tear gas canisters, was that they would be invading the communi-ty preserve of Junín and that those they would find there would not be squatters but members of the local coopera-tive. The day of the takeover, the general also brought along the mining corporation's head of security, in a jeep with five pit-bulls trained to obey his voice and none other. And he crafted the worst plan of attack in history. It was such a disaster that the press soon learned that a group of unarmed peasants had surrounded the paramilitary group during its lunch break, taken possession of their weapons, and locked them up in the local church until the authorities could ar-rive. Since no one wanted to take responsibility for this disaster, the television channels had enough time to arrive and interview the detainees, who explained exactly what Villavicencio had promised them. With that lead, it was not difficult to connect the dots that led from the ex-general to the recent grant of the Eagle I and Eagle II concessions to the Eagle Copper Corporation. As a public relations specialist, the general was a total flop. Holmes immediately called on Vinueza to get them out of this jam, but Andrés was in the final days of a tumultuous and dramatic electoral contest that demanded all his attention, because his candidacy was in danger of dissolving under accusations of unconstitutionality. Still, acutely aware of the importance of the agreements signed with Holmes, he assigned the task of hastening to the area to José María. This struck him, too, as a fine way to divert attention from the way the blind men had been reduced in number after the fatal denouement of their night in the capital. He was fed up with the suspicions of the reporters, who repeatedly demanded to know what had happened to the fifth man. If he sent the remaining four away with José María, people would forget about them until he was in power.

He placed a call to Chicho Salém.

✧ ✧ ✧

"Hey Chicho, hermano, how are you doing?"

"Andrés? Am I speaking to Andrés Vinueza, in the flesh?"

"In the flesh, and needing you on an urgent matter."

"Whatever you need, hermanito, whatever you need. By the way, since I haven't had a chance before, congratulations on your candidacy,."

"That's exactly why I'm calling, because I've got something that needs doing and I can't handle it personally during the election. I need your guys to fix a problem created by a first-class asshole, that's now landed in my lap."

"A problem where?"

"García Moreno. In Intag."

There was an instant's hesitation before the reply.

"I'll go you one better. I'll attend to it myself. I've got something that needs doing with an ex-congressman who

133

lives around there. I'm tired of the way he's been treating me. More than tired, I'm through with it."

"Perfect," Vinueza said, and smiled. "Go to the Eagle Copper Corporation camp tomorrow, where you'll find my associate José María, who'll tell you what to do. And, of course, whatever you want, afterward. Once I'm seated in that yellow velvet chair in the Presidential Palace, anything you want."

✧ ✧ ✧

Relaxed and happy, Benito returned to the apartment at eleven a.m. to find Varas and Valentina asleep on the living room couch, fully dressed and completely entwined, with Témoc watching attentively at their feet. The windows were open, with a gentle breeze lifting the curtains so they billowed like sails on the high seas. Bound for where? He went to the kitchen, made coffee, and set the table. He'd managed to convince the woman at the store that things were about to change and that he'd pay off his and Varas's tabs by the end of the month. For music, he opted for the mellifluous JJ. The album *Sombras* seemed appropriate.

Varas was the first to wake up. He carefully extricated his arm without disturbing Valentina and smiled at his friend. Before saying anything, he went to the bathroom and threw water on his face.

"And where have you been?" he asked once back in the kitchen.

"From what I can see, you ought to be glad I was gone," Benito said.

Varas smiled and poured himself a cup of coffee. He sat down at the table before saying anything else.

"Not really, Benito. I'm done in. I've heard too much. I feel like something is shooting off rockets inside my head."

Benito saw that he'd misread the situation once again. He needed to change the soundtrack to something much more upbeat that could coax a smile from Varas. Jackson do Pandeiro would be perfect. *Forró do Jackson* was an album to cheer the soul, and, in honor of Martirio, the track *a mulher que virou homem*. Two birds with one stone, or almost, anyway.

"Hermano, I leave you alone for a day and a half and come back to find you've turned Cassandra on me. Spit it out. You've got everything you need: a friend, coffee, even a betrayal of Café Tacuba."

Benito had won the battle of tone. He knew that whoever sets the tone leads the conversation where he wants. Varas told him what Valentina had said but managed to skim some of the horror from her words. Words hid as much as they revealed, and while Varas spoke they turned into things that had happened, that was all. Things that had happened to Valentina and a hundred other women. The details were hazy, but there was no need to stir the coals to set them aflame. Not now, not yet.

"So what are we going to do?" Benito asked.

"Go to the public prosecutor and file charges against the blind men."

"And about the women?"

"The police wouldn't go looking for them before. What do you think would happen if we asked them to send a squad into the tunnels?"

"They'd toss you in jail for coming to them with frivolous lies."

Varas nodded and turned to look at Valentina.

"It did her good to talk. I think this is the first time she's slept peacefully since I found her."

"What's her voice like?" Benito asked.

"Like crystal clear water dripping slowly through yards of blue velvet," Varas said.

❖ ❖ ❖

There were fifteen people gathered around the tree, all wearing binoculars on straps around their necks, all with their feet squeezed into rubber boots completely coated with mud. Some held their binoculars at the ready, while others had them up to their eyes. A dozen of the fifteen were in Bermuda shorts; some wore baseball caps and others had sunscreen slathered thickly on their noses. All were completely silent except for one who intermittently blew on a wooden whistle with a loud, high-pitched sound. Their facial expressions suggested mystical rapture or enlightenment, as if a collective epiphany had just occurred. They were looking upward. José María paid them no attention, nor did he turn back to gaze into the upper foliage of the tree. If he had done so, he would have seen a golden crown quetzal in all its magnificent glory. But he wasn't there to birdwatch. His problem was that his car was stuck in a mud bank outside the town of Santa Rosa, and he needed to get to García Moreno before Salém and his hired crew, to tell them what to do. On top of which, here he was bushwhacking alongside the four blind men and an eight-year-old boy, the sole individual who had shown any willingness to guide them. The only thing that helped José María to maintain a degree of composure was the knowledge that, with Salém, he'd be in the hands of a

136

professional—one who would insure his future earnings against the threat of idiotic ecologists.

✧ ✧ ✧

Chicho Salém and his men entered the village of Selva Alegre at midnight to avoid being seen. They headed straight for the Campo Sol hacienda, where they planned to surprise the ex-congressman Robert Bermúdez while he slept—but the house was empty and the surprise was on them. Particularly when they followed the road that led to the Río Pamplona and found sixteen cows riddled with bullets on its shore. Someone had been there before them. Salém was angry, because Bermúdez's disappearance meant he wasn't going to collect the 150,000 euros the ex-legislator owed him. There was no way to collect from the man's family, because the wife and sister were in jail, charged with drug trafficking, and all their possessions were confiscated by the court. Nor could he get his hands on the land through which he and his men were now proceeding, because the titles had been tied up in court ever since the former owners filed charges of extortion against Bermúdez. He decided there was nothing to be done about all this tonight, so at least they should be able to sleep in comfort. He told his men to break down the door to the house. Before heading for the bedrooms, they drank up two bottles of Johnny Walker Black Label they found in the bar. They knew they'd have to wake up early to overtake the man Vinueza had sent to García Moreno, and indeed they did get up before dawn, gather their things, and pile into the double-cab all-terrain pickup parked outside. Then they set off in search of a route that would take them to their rendezvous. But the Lord works in mysterious ways. While they were rounding a sharp curve they met up with a cruiser belonging to the National Police coming in the opposite direction, driven by an officer who'd been assigned the night before to investigate a report of shots fired in Bermúdez's hacienda but had spent much of his time on a binge in Apuela, nearby. The crash sent both vehicles tumbling down the cliff-side until they were swallowed up by the dense foliage of the Intag cloud forest. Neither would ever be seen again, other than by the majestic mountain caracaras, birds of prey whose numbers were already diminishing but who this morning received an unexpected gift, as if from heaven, of rare coastal delicacies soaked in alcohol for their scavenging delight.

The Prosecutor

"This world feeds off those who are sent to the slaughterhouse and those who watch them go by. Those five guys aren't the only guilty parties. They've got plenty of company."

So said Benito while he paced through the apartment, trying to reconcile what he'd just heard with the reality he knew. He'd spent hours in the attempt but hadn't succeeded. "Kidnapping, imprisonment, rape, for years on end . . ."

Benito stopped in mid-sentence and looked toward the sofa where Valentina had been. Then he looked back at Varas.

"So? You're going to have to pull some friend out of your pocket, because going through regular channels won't produce any action," the poet said.

"You think I don't know that?" Varas retorted.

"So?" Benito repeated, pouring his third cup of coffee of the morning.

"Banegas. He's the only one we can count on. He's not the world's most orthodox prosecutor, but he is the only one who can help us. We used to swap copies of *Batman* in school, and I think he took the Caped Crusader's idea of vengeance through justice seriously. He's a good friend, even if he is flamboyant. Back in junior high, he tried to dress like Bogart in *The Maltese Falcon* and he was always a couple of payments behind on the pocket watch with the gold chain. It's still hanging from his belt to this day. He won't hesitate to call out a whole brigade to find the women, or to ask the city for help discovering the tunnels. I'm willing to bet on that."

"But is that enough? Where is he going to put all those women until someone shows up to identify them? If anyone even does ..."

Varas thought that over. The logistics of the operation didn't worry him so much as the Ecuadorian legal system and the way it was applied. He doubted there was any specific law against the crime that had been committed against the women, and, even if there was, would anyone enforce it? But one thing at a time. He called the public prosecutor's office and made an appointment with his childhood friend.

✧ ✧ ✧

José María was late getting into García Moreno, but at least he'd arrived before Salém, so he sat in the plaza to wait. He dismissed the boy and went to the store for some water. Everyone who was out at this hour regarded him and his entourage with suspicion. He hadn't been planning on any bushwhacking, and now his pants were covered in mud, as were his imported leather shoes. He and the blind men were all suffering from one degree or another of sunstroke, though the men seemed unusually alert. Throughout the trek, they'd been talking about angels and heavenly signs. José María had managed to figure out that their celestial beings were in fact the hundreds of birds that flocked to this region. If he had taken the time to study these, he would have realized that they really were from another world. Especially the tanagers, which looked more like apparitions from paradise than earthly birds.

Afternoon came, Salém still had not put in an appearance, and calling his cellphone yielded only dead air. At sunset, the British tour group who had been entranced by the quetzal that morning showed up in the plaza to await the bus that would take them back to Otavalo. José María inquired and found that a gift to their driver, of a monetary sort, would let him and his entourage join in. He didn't see any point in hanging around where they were until after dark, because there was no way he and the blind men were going to spend the night in the mining camp barracks without Salém. The election would happen the next day. There would be nothing to do but follow the news reports and projections. All the polls said Andrés was the sure winner, but of course, it was Andrés who had commissioned them.

✧ ✧ ✧

Varas thought that if you wanted to end your life, there was no need to commit suicide. All you had to do was get yourself trapped someplace like Poso Wells. After his phone call to Banegas he went to see Montenegro to bring the old man up to date. Montenegro did not seem at all stunned, having lived long enough that nothing could surprise him.

But the news did cause him alarm. Weren't those the same men who were now going around with Vinueza? The same ones he'd seen that sleepless night, passing in front of his house? Varas nodded but said nothing more. Benito was still at Varas's apartment with Valentina and Témoc. Once the women were found, Valentina's testimony would be needed, but until then there was no need to submit her to the spectacle that the excavation and search were sure to become. The show would begin as soon as the bulldozers appeared. No doubt about that, because Banegas was an expert in such things. And indeed, that's how it went. The prosecutor arrived at 11 a.m. with a TV crew, a battalion of workers, two bulldozers and a dozen cops. Varas and Montenegro were there, too, both in lightweight cotton pants and short-sleeved shirts. The sun was almost at its zenith, the heat intense, but Banegas had on a black felt sombrero with a silver band and an enormous brim, a black-and-white three-piece suit, sunglasses, cowboy boots, and his ever-present pocket watch and chain. He embraced Varas and asked to be shown the hole leading to the tunnels. Then he climbed onto one of the machines and raised his hand, pointing out where to begin tearing up the ground. Thus he launched one of the most eventful workdays of his career.

✧ ✧ ✧

Holmes was fed up with problems caused by peasants and environmentalists. They were the same all over the world, but he found the Latin Americans to be the most exasperating. They seemed to take every polluted river so much to heart, every animal migration route interrupted, every tree that was felled—as if something inside of them shattered when these things occurred. Plants, insects—some died, others were born, what difference did it make? Latin Americans had no vision of the future. All they knew was how to live in the present. They didn't understand anything about progress, which was why they were in the shape they were in. Nothing could change his opinion that the root cause of their underdevelopment lay in their lack of concentration and inability to project into the future. Letting themselves get sidetracked, they lost their way so easily. Still, though he saw this trait as a defect, he couldn't deny that—in the right circumstances and with the right people—it made his job easier. If some defended a mangrove swamp with their lives, others (again in the right conditions, this was the key) were equally inclined to sell the subsoil rights to their entire country, without hesitation, for the right amount and with minimum benefit to the inhabitants. It was no longer done with colored beads, or even paper money. No, just zerocs and ones flowing through a digital network, moving quantities beyond human imagination from one account to another, from one country to the next. Air—really he trafficked in thin air. He laughed, though nothing was funny. In fact, everything was going poorly. His shares of Barrick Gold had tumbled precipitously after the destruction of Andean glaciers in Pascua Lama, wreaked in pursuit of ten billion dollars' worth of gold, had been called to the attention of the world press by Chilean peasants. And now some sonofabitch radical ecologists were daring to distribute fake nuggets emblazoned with the words "dirty gold." So what if a bit of water got removed from the landscape, when water was everywhere, all around us? What most offended

Holmes's refined and exquisite sense of language was the obvious oxymoron. Gold glowed, gold was perfect; gold was scarce, everyone wanted it. What people want can never be dirty, he thought. It can be many other things, but dirty? No. Gold was beautiful, just like copper. That was its essence. Hadn't Yeats said so? How can we tell the dancer from the dance? And those damn troublemakers in Cotacachi—what good did the forest do them, sitting on millions of dollars in copper? He laughed again. You didn't need much sense of humor to find some amusement in your own troubles, especially when you knew they could be overcome. That's what power was for, to move forward and shake off the debris. And power was something of which he had more than enough.

✧ ✧ ✧

In the mountains, nothing had gone right for José María. Now, on the way to Otavalo, the bus had blown two tires, and why? Because the tourists had insisted on the scenic route, a filthy track little more than a goat path, as José María had thought from the outset. So here they were, with nobody around to help them. The landscape was nothing to write home about, but when one of the twenty Brits announced the sighting of a caracara overhead, the rest forgot the fix they were in and began comparing notes and discussing the characteristics of the animal's flight to ascertain whether it was indeed a kind of falcon or, as the most daring among them maintained, a condor.

"All this fuss about a buzzard," the driver muttered while installing the one spare tire and wondering what to do with the British bird fanatics he was guiding and the five evil-looking men who'd boarded at the last minute in García Moreno.

When he was done, he gathered them all around the bus and explained the situation: no help could reach them because night was already falling, but someone would come early in the morning so that he could get them to Otavalo as planned. Meanwhile he'd managed to get in touch with a friend who lived in a nearby community and was willing to put them up. It wouldn't be like a hotel, but he could promise them dinner and a roof over their heads. Moreover, the dawn would be impressive because they'd be near the Cusín volcano, which along with the Cubilche, the Azaya, the Pangladera, and Cunrru made up the Imbabura volcanic complex, and there was no better vantage point from which to see the northern mountains catching the first rays of the sun. The Brits, enthused, quickly collected their backpacks. José María did not share their excitement.

"How long has it been since those volcanoes erupted?" he wanted to know.

The group was now in motion behind the guide, who answered over his shoulder without stopping.

"A long time. I'm more worried about getting where we're going while we've still got light. But these are young mountains, morphologically speaking, not very worn down by erosion. If I had to predict, I'd say that of all the volcanoes in Ecuador, they're the most dangerous."

After all, the guy had asked.

José María and the blind men, hand in hand, ran after the group before it could disappear over a hill.

XIV

The Sovereign People

For Vinueza, things were going swimmingly. There was his name on all of the ballots that had rolled off the presses of the Instituto Geográfico Militar, now disseminated throughout the national territory. The hand had been dealt, all that remained was to play it. The blind men, as he'd thought, were indeed the ace up his sleeve. He had to thank his father, who, if he hadn't taught him much, had taken care that his son should learn how to pull off a successful bluff. He'd played the past two weeks with his best poker face, and he was getting away with it. He couldn't even believe it himself. It was a perfect union of the human and the divine: his disappearance, his sufferings, his redemption, and then the pardon of his own tormentors. No public relations professional could have dreamed up a better image for the new president of the Ecuadorian people. He had managed to convince, at the least, two million of them. His eyes watered with happiness, imagining all he could do once he reached the presidency. He was happy. He was a truly happy man.

✧ ✧ ✧

"Can you get over here right away?" Varas said into his phone.

"What's happening?" Benito asked, worried.

"Man, where should I start? Banegas insisted on using bulldozers even though I told him that half of the Cooperative was built on top of tunnels and garbage."

"And one of the tunnels collapsed under the machines?"

"*Güey*, you've got a future as a clairvoyant, or writing disaster films. Yes, that's what happened."

"And what do you want me to do?"

"We need to get to work. You told me about that woman around here that everybody respects. Bring her for me to introduce to Banegas. Montenegro already went home because this is turning into a tabloid special. Everyone's screaming, the police are setting up a perimeter and every once in a while the crowd . . ."

"But . . ."

"No more predictions, Benito, go find your Bella and bring her, okay? And what about Valentina? Is she doing okay?"

"She discovered a guitar and she's trying to remember a tune. Take it easy, I'm leaving right now. Témoc will watch her till we come back."

✧ ✧ ✧

When lights glimmered in the distance, the guide relaxed. A family had offered up their house, where a roaring fire in the middle of the single room cast impressive shadows on

148

the adobe walls. Off in one corner, some guinea pigs huddled against the wall. Above the fire hung a pot showing the signs of years spent resisting the flames. Fava beans and corn were boiling in the pot, while a plate on the ground held a large hunk of homemade cheese and a knife. The tourists came in and arranged themselves around the fire, but as soon as the blind men entered, guided by José María, the guinea pigs began emitting high-pitched cries. A man came in and picked up three lifeless bodies. He showed the dead animals to the guide and whispered something in his ear in Quichua, then left. The guide went directly to José María and told him another fire was being built outside for him and the blind men, who couldn't remain in the house. The hooting of an owl could be heard piercing the night.

"What are you talking about?" said José María, annoyed. "We're tired, I just want to lie down in a corner and sleep, then get up early in the morning and leave."

"Guinea pigs are very sensitive animals. Three of them died of fright when you and your companions came in. The community has been very friendly in letting you remain at all, even outside. Please follow me. I'm sure you can get your rest around the other fire."

The fifteen Brits looked at them like they were pariahs. It was late, and José María could smell a hostile environment. He went out, leading the blind men, who had stayed completely silent. The night was immense. It felt as if objects had forgotten their shapes and colors, and everything was on its knees before the enormity of the world. The five men sat around a small fire built on large black stones.

"It's an omen," said one of the men.

"The sacrifice did not come in vain," continued another.

"Lie down and sleep," José María advised imperiously. "Tomorrow you'll have to get up at dawn."

"It's a sign, the spirits are coming from heaven, as in the prophecies and hymns."

José María decided to ignore them. Someone had put out a few donkey hides, so he took one and wrapped himself in it. He smelled something alive, primeval, and distant, but sleep overcame him right away. The blind men didn't sleep. They stood up and walked into the darkness. Before they disappeared, one could be heard saying that the angels would guide them.

✧ ✧ ✧

At Bella's door, Benito could barely stay on his feet. He knocked, and when she opened he said that love was a rebellious bird that no one could trap. He waited for the uncomfortable silence that would follow such an outburst, but Bella responded right away.

"I can lend you some cages," she said, and then she smiled. "I make them myself."

What a woman this was, he thought.

Once she invited him in, Benito told her everything Valentina had recounted. Then he asked for her help in organizing the women's rescue because, from what he understood, things were getting chaotic on the empty lot. So she went with him to the sinister spot, the Bermuda Triangle, the stinking hole at the center of Poso Wells. Indeed all hell was breaking loose. Benito spotted Varas, and they went over to him. Benito did the introductions.

"Who's in charge of this?" Bella asked.

Varas pointed out Banegas, who was bending over to

pick up his sombrero after somebody had taken a swing at him for not being allowed to cross the police line.

"Good afternoon," Bella said.

Banegas looked at Varas, who nodded.

"Do you live here, Señora?" Banegas asked.

"Yes, and if you could be so kind, could you tell me what you're doing?"

"We came to rescue some women."

"Where are you going to put them? Did you bring any clothes so they can cover themselves once they get out? Why don't I see a doctor anywhere? Have you gotten anyone out yet?"

Benito smiled, a big smile that spread across his lips.

"Allow me," Bella said, and took the bullhorn from Banegas's hand. She flipped the switch and turned toward the hundreds of onlookers who had gathered around the lot. "Prosecutor Banegas is here to carry out an investigation, and if you don't let him work in peace, the police presence could go on indefinitely. Do you hear me? Indefinitely. I'm sure he'll keep us informed about what's happening. Isn't that so?" She turned to Banegas, who nodded. "But please, right now, get moving, will you?"

The people began to leave, and Banegas thought to himself how much he needed someone like this in his department. He'd have to talk with her before he left.

"Now, Prosecutor, don't you think you should have some tents put up, for when the women come out? I remember there were some soldiers stationed here during the search for Vinueza. Colonel Alcíbar Peña was in charge of the operation, so he knows the territory. And the Corps of Engineers could speed up the search in the tunnels, don't you think? A call to the Red Cross wouldn't be a bad idea either."

Banegas followed the suggestions and in less than an hour the fallen bulldozer had been retrieved. A Red Cross ambulance arrived, and a surprised Col. Peña found himself taking orders from Bella.

✧ ✧ ✧

The night was peopled with scores of secrets that the men interpreted as they wished while they climbed the lower slopes of the volcano. The four blind men sank into the loose sand as they walked. The sand of an hourglass. They sensed they were moving backward as they neared their ancestral lands. None of them remembered their grandfathers' teachings, since from earliest childhood all they had ever done was repeat the incoherent notions of which they had managed to convince themselves. And now, really, it didn't matter. Their scattered beliefs were nothing in the face of the immense architecture of the universe. They walked for hours, knowing they were lost, until they felt rain on their heads. Except that what was plummeting from the sky was not rain, but birds, falling around the blind men like a torrent of hail. The men didn't run for shelter, there was nowhere to go. They lay down on the ground and covered their faces. And waited for the end of the world.

Which wasn't too far off.

Without You . . .

Vinueza got the call right after voting at his local polling place. José María's voice was breaking up, but from what Vinueza could catch, he'd been arrested, accused of stealing the crown from the statue of Our Lady of Sorrows in the town of Totoras. What the hell was José María doing there, messing around with the local Virgin? Weren't the blind men enough, as far as saints were concerned? He also heard that the four remaining blind men had disappeared, that José María had been searching for them all morning until he'd been detained by the parishioners of the church. Salém had never reached García Moreno, and residents of Junín had taken over the mining facilities. Vinueza turned on the television. None of the channels talked about the elections, only about the orange alert issued by the mayor of Ibarra due to the imminent eruption of the Imbabura volcano. All morning, birds had been falling from the sky around the complex of five volcanoes. The inhabitants had fled as soon as they smelled the gases emerging from various locations of the terrain surrounding the Laguna de

San Pablo. Volcanologists who had hurried to the region were saying that water vapor mixed with sulfur dioxide had condensed into sulfuric acid. The Supreme Electoral Tribunal was considering canceling the elections. If vapor was escaping, this was because some tectonic plate was in motion, which suggested there could be an earthquake of tremendous proportions, releasing lava from the entrails of the volcanos. Whether the gases had all escaped or would mix with the lava, there would be plenty of fireworks either way. Depending on the craters that would form and the weight they could support, the lava flows could reach as far as the coast, and most certainly would cover the land around the volcanoes.

"Intag!" Vinueza thought, and hurried to call Holmes.

✧ ✧ ✧

On Sunday afternoon, Banegas issued statements to the national media that pointed directly to the blind men who had been accompanying Vinueza in his short electoral campaign, implicating them in the kidnapping of more than a hundred women who had now been rescued from the tunnels that lay under the main streets of the slum settlement called Cooperativa Poso Wells, on the southern edge of the country's main port.

"It remains to be seen what other charges may be brought," he went on, appearing next to Bella as they led a group of mud-caked women to the group of tents erected on the vacant lot.

✧ ✧ ✧

"Who is it? Hello? I can barely hear you," said Varas into the static on his cellphone.

"Varitas, don't you recognize my voice? What ingratitude!"

"I seem to recall that you're the editor who fired me from his newspaper," Varas said.

"Always so free in your choice of verbs, Varitas."

"In their appropriate use, Eduardo."

"Listen, could you come to the office? If I remember right, you've got quite a story to tell . . ."

"The one you're watching right now on TV?"

"Such a joker, Varitas . . ."

Varas began inspecting his fingernails and then scraping under them with a toothpick until he heard the man on the other end clear his throat.

"Are you still there?" Eduardo asked nervously.

Varas maintained his silence. After a bit, once assured there was no more dirt under his nails, he replied.

"If there's no eruption, maybe I'll drop by tomorrow around noon."

"Eruption my ass. I just got done interviewing some French experts who say it could be today or it could be in seven hundred and fifty-five years. First thing in the morning, Varitas, first thing in the morning, we'll have to see what happens with the elections . . ."

✧ ✧ ✧

Holmes didn't even bother answering Vinueza's call, because he was boarding a plane for Santiago de Chile. He was taking advantage of being in the same continent to visit the commissioners who had brokered an accord between Chile and Argentina to convert the summit of the Andes—he had enjoyed this description in one particular newspaper—into a virtual country open to multinational mining companies, a sort of no-man's-land without taxes or royalties to pay. He liked it when the press did their work properly. This was an accord, signed and sealed by the two nations, that no one could dismantle. By comparison, the Ecuador thing was still a needle in a haystack. Too many black holes, too many legal vacuums that would interfere with exploiting the mines in peace. But there was no hurry, that was what satellite technology was for. He had at his disposal a map of Ecuador with all the mining deposits highlighted in a full range of brilliant colors—and there were a lot of them. It was just a question of time, of waiting for the right government to come to power, convincing enough investors, publicizing the benefits, and getting the credulous inhabitants of the country to believe in them. He could do all that in a single day's work, but not today, not now, sometime in the future. Ah, the future! The future opened before him, a vast potpourri of opportunities. He found his seat and, once buckled in, asked the stewardess for a glass of champagne.

✧ ✧ ✧

"I don't know, Bella, you tell me. What do I do to stop thinking that?"

Varas smiled. He was riding in the copilot's seat of the taxi taking them home. In back, Benito and Bella were absorbed in a tangled discussion of cages and permissions to do who-knew-what with whatever they had in their heads. The sky was bright blue and the sun was an immense golden ball that cast its light on the city without leaving the tiniest patch of shade in which to take cover or escape. Escape? Escape did not seem to be anyone's priority in this car, as it nosed forward through the packed streets of the center of Guayaquil.

Gabriela Alemán was born in Rio de Janeiro, Brazil, on September 30, 1968, and is the daughter of an Ecuadorian diplomat. She received a PhD at Tulane University and holds a Master's degree in Latin American Literature from Universidad Andina Simón Bolívar. She currently resides in Quito. Her literary honors include: Guggenheim Fellowship in 2006; member of Bogotá 39, a 2007 selection of the most important up-and-coming writers in Latin America in the post-Boom generation; one of five finalists for the 2015 Premio Hispanoamericano de Cuento Gabriel García Márquez (Colombia) for her story collection *La muerte silba un blues*; and winner of several prizes for critical essays on literature and film. Her books include the short story collections *Maldito Corazón* (1996), *Zoom* (1997), *Fuga Permanente* (2002), *La muerte silba un blues* (2014), and *Álbum de familia* (2016); her novels include *Body Time* (2003), *Poso Wells* (2007), and *Humo* (2017).

Dick Cluster has translated four books for City Lights: *In the Cold of the Malecón and Other Stories* (2000) by Antonio José Ponte, *Frigid Tales* (2002) by Pedro de Jesús, *A Corner of the World* (2014) by Mylene Fernández-Pintado, and *Poso Wells* (2018) by Gabriela Alemán. His own novels include *Return to Sender* (1990), *Repulse Monkey: Book 2 in the Alex Glauberman Mystery Series* (2015), and *Obligations of the Bone: Book 3 in the Alex Glauberman Mystery Series* (2015).